He had ▮▮▮▮▮▮
others could ▮▮▮ ▮▮▮▮▮
about, and they
envied him.

Was that why Ambrose Kerr held people at arm's length? Emilie had assumed that he would never want her, because she was so young and naive.

But then she discovered the reason Ambrose was so wary—he hid an incredible secret. The truth only made Emilie want Ambrose more, but it was also *dynamite!*

If others got to know the real story, the new-found happiness of Emilie and Ambrose would explode....

Dear Reader,

The Seven Deadly Sins are those sins that most of us
are in danger of committing every day: very ordinary
failings, very human weaknesses, which can
sometimes cause pain to both ourselves and others.
Over the ages they have been defined as Anger,
Covetousness, Envy, Greed, Pride, Lust and Sloth.

In this book I deal with the sin of Envy. We all dream
about having lots of money, or being beautiful, or
blissfully happy with a man we love, and it is natural
to envy someone else who seems to have what we only
dream about. Envy can poison life, though, if it isn't
kept under control. It could even lead to tragedy.

Charlotte Lamb

This is the third story in Charlotte Lamb's gripping
seven-part series, SINS. Watch out from now until
December for another SINS story every month.

Coming next month: *Wild Hunger*...the sin of Greed.
Have you ever had too much of a good thing?

ALSO AVAILABLE FROM HARLEQUIN PRESENTS

SINS
1816—SECRET OBSESSION: the Sin of Pride
1822—DEADLY RIVALS: the Sin of Covetousness

Don't miss any of our special offers. Write to us at the
following address for information on our newest releases.

Harlequin Reader Service
U.S.: 3010 Walden Ave., P.O. Box 1325, Buffalo, NY 14269
Canadian: P.O. Box 609, Fort Erie, Ont. L2A 5X3

Charlotte Lamb

Haunted Dreams

Harlequin Books

TORONTO • NEW YORK • LONDON
AMSTERDAM • PARIS • SYDNEY • HAMBURG
STOCKHOLM • ATHENS • TOKYO • MILAN
MADRID • WARSAW • BUDAPEST • AUCKLAND

If you purchased this book without a cover you should be aware that this book is stolen property. It was reported as "unsold and destroyed" to the publisher, and neither the author nor the publisher has received any payment for this "stripped book."

ISBN 0-373-11828-7

HAUNTED DREAMS

First North American Publication 1996.

Copyright © 1995 by Charlotte Lamb.

All rights reserved. Except for use in any review, the reproduction or utilization of this work in whole or in part in any form by any electronic, mechanical or other means, now known or hereafter invented, including xerography, photocopying and recording, or in any information storage or retrieval system, is forbidden without the written permission of the publisher, Harlequin Enterprises Limited, 225 Duncan Mill Road, Don Mills, Ontario, Canada M3B 3K9.

All characters in this book have no existence outside the imagination of the author and have no relation whatsoever to anyone bearing the same name or names. They are not even distantly inspired by any individual known or unknown to the author, and all incidents are pure invention.

This edition published by arrangement with Harlequin Books S.A.

® and TM are trademarks of the publisher. Trademarks indicated with ® are registered in the United States Patent and Trademark Office, the Canadian Trade Marks Office and in other countries.

Printed in U.S.A.

CHAPTER ONE

'LET'S get married, Em!'

'Sholto!'

The soft gasp was incredulous, more horrified than delighted. The man eavesdropping couldn't help smiling, although he had been irritated when he heard the other two walk in here. They had no idea he was there, of course. The room was shadowy, just one lamp lit on a small low table behind him. He had a headache threatening; light made it worse, as did the constant babble of voices, the throb of music, in the party going on outside. That was why he had retreated into this room, which was his study. As the host he ought to be out there, talking to people.

Moving warily a fraction, he could see the intruders in a mirror on the wall above him.

They still hadn't noticed him; he had his back to them and was hidden by the deep leather armchair he sat in, for one thing, and, for another, they were far too absorbed in themselves.

He could only see the boy in profile, but the girl was facing him; he saw the dim light glimmering on sleek brown hair, on a string of pearls around a pale, slender throat, on wide, startled blue eyes.

'I'm serious! I'm crazy about you, you know I am—oh, come on, Em, say yes!' The boy was excited, a little drunk, his voice furry, thickened. 'We can get engaged tonight... Announce it here, tell everyone... That would make them all sit up!'

He had shifted, coming full-face. Their audience realised then that this was no boy. He recognised him— he should have picked up on the name at once; it was hardly a common one. Sholto Cory must be in his twenties, surely? Much older than the girl with him, anyway. Blond hair, blue eyes, a fresh complexion, he was attractive and lively, and led a busy social life. The youngest son of a Scottish family with land, but not much money, he was lucky enough to have brains. He had gone into banking and was doing well, but there was a question mark against him in the mind of the man watching him. Was Sholto tough enough to claw his way to the top?

The watcher's narrowed grey eyes moved to assess the girl again. He was sure he had never seen her before. Small, slender, with a fall of straight dark brown hair, well-brushed and shining, a cool oval face, and big, blue, dreamy-looking eyes with incredibly long dark lashes, she wasn't pretty, certainly not beautiful, and wore very little make-up, compared with some of the other female guests tonight. From the look of her, she had only just left school. Pale pink lipstick on her mouth, a dusting of powder on her small nose... Those lashes were real, and she wore no eyeshadow.

It surprised him that Sholto Cory should have fallen for a girl like this—he would have expected Sholto to go for something more obvious, a glitzy type. Sholto must have better taste than he had ever suspected.

But the girl had a sort of radiance; her nature shone in her face, in her gentle blue eyes, the sweet curve of her mouth. Her party dress was a pansy-blue silk, demure, almost old-fashioned, but it suited her perfectly, and the cut made him suspect it had been designed for her by someone very clever and very expensive.

He even thought he could name the designer—her clients tended to be conservative and very rich—which meant that this girl must come from a wealthy family. Did that explain Sholto's interest?

His mouth twisted wryly. Or am I just too cynical? he wondered.

'You're not serious, Sholto!' the girl was saying.

'Of course I am!' Sholto retorted, sounding impatient, then dived at her and began trying to kiss her.

'Oh, don't!' She wriggled away, shaking her head. 'Sholto, I can't... I'm sorry, I don't want to hurt your feelings, but I really can't... I do like you, you know I do, but marriage... No, I'm not ready to get married yet.'

'We don't have to get married for ages! We could just get engaged.'

'If we get engaged they'll all start planning the wedding, and before we know where we are they'll fix a date and... Oh, I can't, Sholto!'

'I thought you loved me!'

Sholto sounded as if he might start crying, and the girl heard it, looking up at him, her lower lip caught between two rows of small white teeth.

'I'm sorry... Oh, poor Sholto,' she said unhappily.

The man eavesdropping couldn't help smiling again, but Sholto was not amused. She had hurt him—and now she was making it worse by sounding sorry for him!

He went red and grabbed her by the shoulders, pushed her backwards until she met the wall, held her there with his strong, slim body and began to kiss her angrily, bruising her mouth.

She tried to fight him off, but Sholto was stronger; his hands tightened on her, his fingers digging into her soft skin.

'Don't, Sholto! You're hurting me...' she cried in a smothered voice, a sob in her throat.

The man in the armchair hadn't meant to intervene. In fact, he was surprised to find himself on his feet, but he didn't stop to think about what he was doing. He was across the room before they heard him coming. A tall, hard man, he took Sholto by the neck as easily as if he were a puppy and flung him aside.

Sholto fell against the door with a loud crash. 'What the hell...?' he spluttered, recovering almost at once and leaping back towards the other man.

At that instant the older man flicked down a switch on the wall and the chandelier in the centre of the room flooded them all with blinding light.

Sholto stopped dead, his indrawn breath very audible. 'Sir!' He turned white.

The other man ignored him; he was looking at the girl, who was silently crying, tears rolling down her face.

'Are you OK?' he asked her gently.

She didn't answer, just put her hands over her face, trembling so much she had to lean on the wall to stay upright.

Sholto stammered, 'I h-had no idea you were in here, sir. I'm s-sorry if we intruded, we thought the room was empty.'

'Clearly.' The voice was clipped, curt, the man's lips barely parted to let the word out. 'Go back to the party, Cory,' he added.

Sholto looked relieved and gabbled, 'Yes, sir, of course. Come on, Em!'

The other man's voice cracked like a whip. 'Leave her here—she can't go back to the party in that state!'

Sholto hesitated, reddening, met the hard stare of grey eyes and almost ran out of the room, the heavy mahogany door closing behind him with a solid sound.

Pulling a clean white handkerchief out of a pocket, the other man put it into the girl's hand.

She whispered, 'Thank you,' and dried her face, blew her nose, gave him a fleeting glance through those long, long damp lashes, her eyes dark blue with distress and embarrassment.

'I'm sorry we disturbed you.' She began to move sideways towards the door. 'I'll leave you in peace.'

He put a hand out to stop her, not touching her but barring her way. 'I shouldn't go back just yet. Give yourself a minute to calm down before you have to face the others.'

'I am really perfectly well now, but thank you for being so thoughtful.' The grave courtesy was touching; a child playing at being grown-up. How old was she? he wondered. And who was she?

'We ought to introduce ourselves,' he said. 'My name is Kerr.' He watched her, wondering how she would react when she realised who he was. 'Ambrose Kerr.'

The girl's head jerked up, the blue eyes wider than ever, and he noticed how clear the whites were around the sky-colour of the iris; he was reminded of the blue and white sheen of early Chinese porcelain. She stared at him and this time really took in what he looked like, her gaze searching his face. 'Oh,' she said huskily, then, thinking aloud, 'This is your house, then!' Her fine dark brows met. 'It's your party,' she worked out, looking shocked. 'Oh. That's why Sholto looked so horrified.'

Ambrose Kerr's mouth twisted in sardonic amusement, remembering Sholto's face. 'Yes, I don't imagine he was pleased to see me.'

She looked up at him, frowning. 'You should have let us know you were in here as soon as we came in!' she reproached, and he gave her a wry look.

'I apologise, but it all happened so quickly—you came in without warning, and before I could announce my presence Sholto proposed, and I didn't like to interrupt and ruin what could have been a magic moment.'

The dry tone made her turn bright pink. 'Oh...you heard that?'

His grey eyes were amused. 'I'm afraid so. Very reluctantly, I assure you.'

She gave a long groan. 'Sholto will want to die when he realises! Oh, poor Sholto. And he was so thrilled to get the invitation to your Christmas party; he said it was a tremendous compliment to get one.'

He held a party for his staff every Christmas, at his impressive, Nash-designed home in Regent's Park, within a mile of the city headquarters of the bank he ran. He didn't draw up the list of guests himself—the invitations went out on the advice of the senior staff, so that the chairman could meet promising newcomers and assess them in a social situation, and meet again older members of the staff he did not normally come in contact with. Ambrose Kerr knew that they all hoped the party would give them a chance to catch his eye and impress him, and he could imagine how Sholto Cory's heart must have sunk when he recognised him a few moments ago.

'Oh, dear,' the girl said, frowning at nothing, talking in a low, worried voice, as if to herself more than him. 'I feel worse now, but how was I to guess he would propose? Out of the blue, like that?'

Ambrose Kerr watched her, fascinated by the changing expressions on that oval face. She showed everything, didn't she? Colour swept over her face all the time—

now pearly white, now carnation-pink...and those big eyes were revealing too, giving away all her thoughts and feelings. He had never met anyone so transparent, so unprotected, so vulnerable. She shouldn't be let out on her own, he thought; this was not a safe world for innocents, she could get hurt, and he felt a strange pang at that idea. He wasn't usually so protective in his reactions; it startled him to feel that way about this girl. Why had she got under his skin? he wondered, staring at her.

'How long have you been seeing Sholto?' he asked.

She didn't need to think about it. 'Since September the third,' she said at once, and she was smiling suddenly, her eyes bright with memory, making him wonder exactly how she did feel about Sholto Cory. Maybe she liked him more than she realised?

'We met on a river-boat,' she said. 'Going down the Thames to Greenwich on a rainy Saturday; it poured, all day. Everyone else was terribly cross; they were soaked to the skin and some of them had come dressed up in such pretty clothes. They huddled in the bar, drinking, and looking really fed-up. But Sholto was such fun, he made me laugh all the time. We got the giggles and that made everyone else get even crosser.'

It sounded very uncomfortable and far from fun. Ambrose gave her a dry look. 'What on earth were you doing on a river-boat on a rainy day, anyway?'

'Oh, didn't I say? It was a birthday party for Sholto's cousin Julia. I went to school with her, that's why I was invited. It was the first time I'd met Sholto, though. He asked me to go riding with him the next morning; it was a Sunday and he wasn't going to work. He said he would book us a couple of horses from a stable in Epping Forest, and he'd pick me up and drive us out there—it was only a half-hour drive from where I live. He said it was bound to be fine next morning, after all that rain, by the law of averages, and he was right. It was a glorious autumn morning, all the trees in the forest were turning yellow, and we had a wonderful ride. The leaves kept falling all around us, like golden confetti.'

'It sounds very romantic,' he said drily. In fact, it sounded as if she did like Sholto rather more than she realised. Sholto might have been a little too precipitate but perhaps she intended to marry him in the end? It wasn't his business, he knew nothing about her—it didn't matter to him whether or not she married Sholto Cory.

But his frown deepened, carving heavy lines in his brows, lines which had a permanent look, as if he frowned a good deal, thought the girl, watching him. Not because he was bad-tempered, she decided, her eye wandering over the rest of his strong, controlled face. There was a faintly sardonic humour about his eyes, a warmth to his mouth—no, he didn't look bad-tempered. He must have a lot on his mind all the time, though.

She knew from Sholto how important he was, how much power he had; she had been curious about him for ages, and now she was impressed—who wouldn't be?

'And you've been seeing Sholto ever since?'

'Well, we're in the same crowd, we see each other at the same parties and so on...yes...'

'But you weren't expecting him to propose?'

'It never entered my head. We barely——' She broke off, a vivid red. 'Well, I mean...I'm not... We aren't... We never...'

He was filling in the blank spaces, his dark brows raised. 'You aren't in love with him?'

Just as obviously, they had never made love either; apart from the odd kiss, he suspected. That was what she couldn't bring herself to say. She's a virgin, he thought, looking into those blue eyes, startled. As rare as a unicorn these days. I don't believe it.

'How old are you?'

She gave him a stricken look, obviously understanding why he asked the question.

'Twenty,' she said half-defiantly. 'Twenty-one in a few months. On the second of April, actually—I just missed April Fool's Day.' She laughed, but Ambrose didn't.

He felt a strange stirring inside his chest, as if he had swallowed a bird that was trying to escape, wings fluttering against his ribs.

I must be sickening for something, he thought—maybe that headache is a symptom of something worse on the way? The last thing I need is to go down with the flu, especially of the virulent kind.

The silence that had fallen had made the girl look nervous. Noticing this, Ambrose said idly, 'Has Sholto been your only boyfriend?' and then wondered what on earth he was doing, asking this total stranger such a question. Serve him right if she slapped his face or walked off in a huff.

She gave him an even more startled look, very flushed, and opened her mouth to answer.

Ambrose quickly said, 'Sorry, not my business, of course.'

'Well, no, it isn't,' she said quietly. 'And I shouldn't have talked about Sholto behind his back, especially to you—he wouldn't like it.'

'No, of course, you're quite right. I'm sorry,' he said gravely.

Sholto must be worried stiff in case he had bitterly offended the very man he most wanted to impress. Ambrose Kerr felt a twinge of pity for him. This wasn't

Sholto's night, was it? And he must have hoped it would be! He had probably planned that proposal, had wanted to do it here, so that he could announce it tonight, in front of the most important people at the bank!

He was probably hanging around outside, watching the door to this room, waiting on tenterhooks for her to come out so that he could pounce and find out what had been said about him in here.

'Please...'

Ambrose looked down at the girl, who gave him a pleading look.

'Yes?'

'Please, could you forget you saw us? That it ever happened, I mean? You won't let it influence you? Against Sholto, I mean... That would be so unfair.'

Still speaking gravely, he promised, 'His career won't suffer. Don't worry.'

Looking at him uncertainly, she asked, 'You promise?'

'I promise,' he said, and smiled at her suddenly, making her blink with surprise at the charm in that smile.

Charm wasn't the first thing you thought about when you looked at Ambrose Kerr. He had an air of authority, calm self-assurance. He was a big man, broad-shouldered, tall, his body fit and powerful. His grey eyes made her shiver a little when they weren't smiling. For all that charm, she didn't think it would be wise to make him really angry. No wonder poor Sholto had looked witless when he recognised him.

Sholto was always talking about him—he admired him from a distance, because of course he didn't know him, had never met him before tonight. Mind you, nobody seemed to know much about Ambrose Kerr, Sholto said.

He had come out of nowhere, shooting across the sky of the business world like a comet over the past decade.

He had no family connections, no history he talked about, and people were far too nervous of him to go on asking questions he made it plain he didn't want to answer.

He had an American background, but he didn't have an American accent. He looked Mediterranean, if anything, with olive skin, close-shaven tonight along that tough jaw; his hair was dark too, smooth, a glossy blue-black in this light, brushed back from a widow's peak, but with a silver streak at the temples.

She could see why he impressed Sholto so deeply. He impressed her. Her nerves rippled; no, it was more than that—he... She frowned, searching for the right word. Disturbed, she thought; that was it. He disturbed her. In fact, being with him was like standing on the very edge of a volcano. You were always aware of depths you couldn't see but which you sensed were explosive and potentially deadly.

'I really must go,' she said uneasily.

'You haven't told me *your* name yet.'

'Emilie,' she said, and spelt it out. 'Emilie Madelin.'

The name meant nothing to him. He repeated it, to memorise it, and at that instant the telephone on the library table began to ring. Ambrose frowned; he had been expecting the call tonight, another reason why he had come into this room—to wait for it.

'I'll have to take that—excuse me for a moment...'

He had meant her to wait, but as he picked up the phone the girl took the opportunity to slip away before he could stop her, murmuring politely, 'Thank you again...'

The heavy mahogany door closed behind her.

Staring at it, Ambrose spoke into the phone curtly. 'Yes?'

'Ambrose?'

'Hello, Gavin. How did it go?'

'Like a dream. We've got him; everything's in place for the kill. You can close in at the board-meeting on Thursday.'

Gavin Wheeler's voice was excited, a little thick, as if he had been drinking, and no doubt he had. Gavin drank far too much, especially when he was coming to the end of a particular project.

Ambrose never drank with him, which, he knew, Gavin resented. From the occasional curious remark, Ambrose knew Gavin suspected him of being a reformed alcoholic, which was ironic. Ambrose's childhood had been made miserable by an alcoholic father who was violent when he was drunk and morose when he was sober. That was why Ambrose himself only drank the occasional glass of wine, on social occasions, and no spirits at all, and never drank when he was alone. But he had never talked to Gavin about his father— Ambrose wasn't giving Gavin any power over him, if he could help it. He did not entirely trust Gavin; in fact, Ambrose did not trust anyone unreservedly.

Coolly, Ambrose said, 'Good work, Gavin. Sure Rendell doesn't have a clue what we're doing?'

'Not unless someone has told him since this morning,' Gavin said, laughing. 'I've personally talked to all the shareholders; their shares will change hands on Thursday, too late for George Rendell to guess what's going on. Our friends on the board all agree that he's too old for the job now. He should have retired long ago.'

'If he'd had a son he would have done, no doubt,' Ambrose said. 'It must have been a terrible blow to him to have no heir.'

'Don't waste any pity on the old man; he has plenty of money to make his retirement comfortable,' Gavin retorted.

'It is still going to hit him hard; his life is invested in that company.' Ambrose rather liked the old man, and was sorry for him, but the company was going downhill when it should be doing well in the current climate, and, with the bank's money invested, it was his duty to make sure their money was safe.

'He'd have to retire soon, anyway,' said Gavin indifferently. He didn't care two pins about George Rendell—he barely knew him. Gavin didn't work at the bank; he was directly responsible to Ambrose, who kept him moving between the bank's clients, doing deals, arranging take-overs, finding out information and researching possible mergers. Gavin was a clever accountant; he had a cold heart and a cool head and the temperament to enjoy following a difficult trail to track down a target.

'He isn't a friend of yours, is he?'

'Not a personal friend, but he has been a client of the bank for a long time.' Ambrose was irritated by the question. Personal feelings couldn't come into the way he dealt with clients. The bank's money had to be safeguarded, that was his job, and they had invested quite a sum in George Rendell's company.

George Rendell's family had been making paper for over a century and had several mills in Kent and Sussex. Two years ago George had asked if he could borrow money with which to update machinery, and Ambrose had agreed, but although George had kept up the monthly repayments, a large amount of the money was still outstanding and the company's audit last year had revealed that, far from an improvement in sales, there had been a falling-off since the new machinery was introduced. Ambrose had come to the conclusion that the management was set in a rut, starting at the top, with George Rendell himself. He was nearing seventy and had no son to take over, allowing him to retire. The company was ripe for take-over. It was in the bank's interest to arrange one with a client firm, safeguarding the bank's investment.

'The company should be making twice the amount of product; the whole place needs a good shake-up,' Ambrose said. 'OK. So when do you fly back?'

'Ten tomorrow.' Gavin had been up to Scotland to see a big shareholder in Rendell and Son who was prepared to sell to their prospective buyer for the firm.

'You've got your secretary with you?'

'She's here right now,' Gavin said, laughing in a way that told Ambrose that the two of them were in bed together.

Gavin always had affairs with his secretaries; he chose them for their looks as much as their brains, although the girls always had both. Gavin expected his secretary to work hard, to be ultra-efficient, as well as good in bed. They never lasted long; about a year was the usual time one stayed with him. Ambrose wasn't sure whether he sacked them or they left, but they kept changing.

Well, he's good at his job, I don't have to like him, thought Ambrose. The way he lives is none of my business.

'Well, work on your report with her during the flight back,' he said coolly. 'Get her to type it up as soon as you arrive, and have it on my desk before five tomorrow.'

'OK. Will you be around when I arrive?'

'No, I have meetings all afternoon, but I'll be back by five. I'll see you then. Goodnight, Gavin, and thank you.'

Ambrose hung up and looked at his watch. The party would soon be over, his guests would start drifting away in half an hour; he had better get out there and circulate for the last few moments.

As soon as he opened the door he was engulfed by people eager for a chance to talk to him. He was just working out how to escape again, when he was rescued by Sophie Grant, one of his senior stock-market experts. She joined the circle surrounding him, waited her moment, and then asked him to show her his latest prize orchid in the heated greenhouse behind the house.

Several others clamoured to see it, but Ambrose explained politely that there should never be more than two people in the orchid-house at a time.

'It uses up too much oxygen,' he assured them.

As he and Sophie walked off she laughed softly. 'What a smooth liar you are!'

Ambrose gave her an amused look. 'An essential tool in the banker's weaponry. And it's true—it isn't a good idea to have too many people in the orchid-house at one time. Thanks for rescuing me, anyway. Do you really want to see the orchids?'

'Of course I do! They fascinate me; there's something luscious and terrible about them. They're so beautiful, yet they look as if they might eat people.'

Ambrose gave her another sideways glance; there was something orchidaceous about Sophie: she was beautiful and looked as if she might eat people—men, anyway! She had thick, white, perfect skin, dark, gleaming eyes and a ripe, full red mouth. Her body was just as extravagant: ultra-female, rounded, sensual, almost de-

fiantly flaunted in the clinging black satin backless dress
with the neckline plunging between her full breasts.

They had had an affair briefly, two years ago. Ambrose
had been attracted, even fascinated, for a brief time but
had soon realised that he didn't like what he found under
the come-hither smile and the desirable body. Sophie was
ambitious and hard-edged; there was no emotion in their
lovemaking, apart from lust, and Ambrose wanted far
more than that from the woman in his life.

He had discreetly backed off, gradually stopped
ringing her, asking her out, and Sophie had accepted it
without a word. He was grateful to her for that. He'd
been afraid she might make a scene, try to hold on to
him. He was convinced she cared no more for him than
he did for her, but he also suspected she had been hoping
to marry him. He had money and social cachet, and
Sophie wanted both. But she hadn't fought for him. She
had behaved impeccably. He had promoted her a few
months later, not a reward for good behaviour, simply
that her tact and discretion had proved to him how
valuable she could be to the bank.

'How's Gavin doing on the Rendell project?' she
asked, when they were in the hot greenhouse looking at
the massed orchids. He had been collecting them for
some years, but lately he no longer found them exciting,
and was considering selling them to the friend who had
talked him into having his own orchid-house.

'Everything's set for the board-meeting on Thursday.'

'Good,' Sophie said, her eyes gleaming. 'I know I
don't usually sit in on board-meetings, but could I come
along on Thursday?'

Ambrose frowned. Sophie was the executive responsible for dealing with the Rendell account, admittedly.
In fact, looking back, he seemed to recall it had been

Sophie who first suggested that they should get someone else in to run the company.

'I don't think that would be appropriate, do you? Aren't you related to the Rendell family, Sophie?'

She gave him another of her cat-like smiles. 'My mother is old George's cousin, but our side of the family have no money. We see very little of the mill people; we aren't good enough for them.' She gazed at the rich patina on a purple orchid. 'Gorgeous thing,' she said in a soft, creamy voice. 'What a pity they don't have any scent.'

What was she thinking about? Not the orchid, Ambrose decided, watching her. Whatever it was, that smile made him uneasy. It made no difference to him whether or not she liked her Rendell relatives—his decision had been based purely on financial grounds—but maybe he shouldn't have given that account to her to manage. He hadn't realised at the time that she had any connection with the Rendells; George himself had mentioned that to Ambrose some months back.

The heat in the greenhouse was beginning to make his shirt stick to his back and sweat was trickling down his neck.

'We had better go back to the party,' he said, making for the door into the house.

People started leaving once he reappeared. Ambrose stood by the front door, shaking hands with departing guests; when Sophie said goodnight he lightly kissed her cheek, and she gave him a tilted, cat-like smile.

'Lovely party, Ambrose. You made us all feel so welcome—you're good at that.'

He heard the sting under the sweetness; he smiled back at her without warmth.

'Thank you. Goodnight, Sophie.'

Sholto had left much earlier; he had said goodnight without meeting his host's eyes and rushed off, alone. Presumably the girl had gone home already, Ambrose had decided, but a few minutes later Emilie Madelin came along the panelled hall towards him, her hand threaded through someone's arm in an intimate, confiding way.

Who was she with now? Ambrose glanced at the man quickly, and did a double-take, stiffening as he saw the grizzled hair, the lined face and pale blue eyes of George Rendell.

George Rendell? Why was the girl with him?

The old man smiled cheerfully at him. 'A very enjoyable evening, Ambrose, as usual. Good of you to invite me. I'm sorry not to have had a chance to talk to you, but with so many people here it was hard to get anywhere near you! Anyway, we enjoyed ourselves, didn't we, Emilie?' He paused as Ambrose stared at the girl. 'Of course, you weren't around when we arrived. I haven't had a chance to introduce her—this is my granddaughter, Emilie.'

Granddaughter. Ambrose turned his stare to Emilie Madelin's gentle face, feeling a strange sickness inside his stomach. There's something wrong with me, he thought. I've been feeling weird all evening. Have I picked up some bug? There was a viral infection going through the staff at the bank at the moment. Maybe that's it, he thought irritably. I haven't got time to be ill!

The girl gave him her grave smile, her blue eyes serious.

Automatically, Ambrose held out his hand. 'I hope you enjoyed the party, Emilie.'

Her hand was small and cool; his swallowed it.

'Very much, thank you, Mr Kerr,' she said in that soft, grave voice. 'You have a beautiful home.'

'You must have dinner with us soon, Ambrose,' George Rendell said.

Ambrose detached his stare from her face. He smiled at the old man. 'I'd like that, thank you,' he said, but his mind was in confusion. She was George Rendell's granddaughter?

Why hadn't he picked up on the name when she spelt it out for him? It was unusual enough, God knew.

He must have the name on file somewhere. He knew that her mother, Rendell's only child, had married a Frenchman and gone to live in France, had had, in her turn, only one daughter, and had then died of cancer at a tragically early age.

The father had been a flamboyant journalist in Paris; he had remarried rather soon afterwards, his new wife had had other children, and this girl had been sent to a French boarding-school. Ambrose hadn't realised that she was now living in England with her grandfather; he had assumed she still lived in France. Why hadn't Gavin found that out? Or had he? But if he had, why wouldn't he have mentioned the fact?

Ambrose knew all about her, on paper; he had even seen a photo of her, he suddenly realised, but it must have been taken some years ago. She had been a schoolgirl in a very neat green and gold uniform. Her large-brimmed hat had half hidden her face, but he had a feeling she had been rather plump and had worn her hair in two long braids tied with green ribbon and hanging right down to her waist.

She looked very different now.

'We're having a dinner party next Tuesday—just a few friends, you'll know most of them, I expect. Short notice,

I know. I don't suppose you're free, but if you are...'
George Rendell paused expectantly, smiling, clearly expecting a polite refusal.

'I think I am,' said Ambrose. He thought he had another dinner engagement, with visiting clients, but that was easy to rearrange; someone else could stand in for him.

But why am I accepting? he asked himself silently. This is crazy. Aloud, though, he said, 'I'd be delighted to have dinner, George, thank you.'

'Well, that's wonderful. Look forward to seeing you then—I don't think we've had you at the house before, have we? Should have thought of it a long time ago, but I haven't entertained much in recent years. Gave all that up after my wife died; been a bit of a recluse, I suppose. All that's changed since Emilie came to live with me.' George looked down at his granddaughter, smiling. 'She's given me a new lease of life. I've started giving dinner parties again, filling the house with young people.'

Ambrose smiled back at him, faintly touched by the old man's fond gaze at the girl.

He was very well-preserved for a man of seventy; upright, active, with a healthy colour in his face. Ambrose knew he went to work each weekday morning at eight, as he always had, and was at his desk until after six. He still had plenty of energy, obviously, but perhaps he no longer cared whether or not the mills were working at maximum efficiency? Perhaps all his attention now was given to this girl?

'We have a town house in Chelsea,' George Rendell said. 'Your secretary will give you the address, I'm sure. You must have it on file. I know how efficient your office is! Off the Embankment, not far from Carlyle's house. Easy to find... Shall we say seven-thirty?'

Ambrose nodded. 'Seven-thirty.'

'Goodnight, then.'

George shepherded the girl in front of him; she gave Ambrose a fleeting smile and he watched them disappear into the winter night, his face pale and his eyes grim.

I shouldn't have accepted that invitation, he thought. This time next week that old man is going to hate my guts; the girl will too. I have no business eating their food, sitting at their table, when I am about to pull the roof down on top of them both.

An hour later Ambrose was in bed, the lights off, the room dark and quiet, the only noises the wind rattling the bare branches of trees in Regent's Park, which he could see from his bedroom, and the unearthly sounds of animals in the zoo on the further side of the park. He normally went to sleep the minute his head hit the pillow. Tonight, though, sleep evaded him until the early hours of the morning. He couldn't remember the last time his conscience had given him that much trouble.

CHAPTER TWO

EMILIE woke up early on Tuesday to a calm, quiet winter morning, the sun hidden behind cloud, a pale lavender light drifting over the walls of her bedroom.

She yawned, thought drowsily, Something special is happening today, and then she remembered. Ambrose Kerr was coming to dinner.

Somewhere there was a rapid noise, a drumming beat. For a second she couldn't think what it was, then she realised that it was her heart, beating faster than the speed of light.

She jumped out of bed and ran into the bathroom to have a shower. In the mirror on the wall she saw her reflection: over-bright eyes, flushed face, a pink, parted mouth breathing fast.

What's the matter with you? she accused herself, then looked away, hurriedly pulled her nightie over her head, the movement tightening her slender body, making her breasts lift, their pink nipples harden and darken against the creamy flesh surrounding them. My breasts are too small! she thought, staring at them. I wish I had a better figure. I wish I had blonde hair—or jet-black? Anything but brown. I wish my hair was naturally curly, too, instead of straight. And oh! I wish I had bigger breasts...

She stepped under the warm jets of water, closing her eyes, and began washing, smoothly lathering her body. Her truant mind kept conjuring up disturbing images. How would it feel to have a man touching her like this? Male hands stroking her shoulders, her throat, her breasts. No, not just any man...Ambrose Kerr. Ever since Saturday night she hadn't been able to stop thinking about him. Her nipples ached, her mouth was dry.

Are you crazy? she asked herself, even pinker now, and breathing twice as fast. He's almost twice your age, sophisticated, very experienced...he wouldn't even look at you!

'How old is he?' she had asked her grandfather as they drove back from Ambrose's home on Saturday, and Grandpa had shrugged indifferently.

'Must be getting on for forty now, I suppose.'

She had realised he must be much older than she was, but...forty? She had sighed. Her father wasn't much older than that!

'Late thirties, anyway,' Grandpa had said, and that sounded much better. Her spirits had lifted.

She had let a minute pass before asking, in what she hoped was an idle, offhand way, 'Has he got children? I suppose there is a Mrs Kerr?'

'I've never heard of one. Plenty of women in his life, though, if you believe the gossips. Sophie was one of them, I gather.'

Emilie had felt a stab of shock. 'Sophie?'

Sophie? Sophie and him? she had thought, shaken and dismayed. She had had no idea. Sophie had never said a word to her about him, but then Sophie never said much about her private life to Emilie.

'They were seen around together for a few months,' George Rendell had said. 'Then it fizzled out, and I would put money on it that it wasn't Sophie who backed off.'

Emilie had stared out of the window, biting her lip. 'Do you think she's in love with him?'

Grandpa's voice had been dry. 'I think she fancied being Mrs Kerr.' He could be quite cynical at times, and Emilie had frowned. Grandpa had continued, 'Sophie takes after her mother, my cousin Rosa. They use their heads, not their hearts, those two women. So sharp they could cut themselves, both of them.'

'I like them both,' Emilie had said quietly, and her grandfather had given her a very different look, his face softening. She'd smiled at him and said, 'Sophie and her mother have been very kind to me.'

She would always be grateful to them for their friendliness when she had first arrived in England.

Her father's family had never been very interested in her and, now that he had sons, neither was her father. A hardbitten journalist, he had never spent much time at home even before her mother died. He had remarried shockingly soon after that.

Emilie suspected that he had been having an affair with Marie-Claude while her mother was alive. Had her mother known about it? She flinched at the thought.

Maman had never said a word to her, if she had known—but when she hadn't known you were looking, the sadness in her face could have wrung your heart. Her mother had had so much to bear: a long, painful illness, which she knew would end in death, made harder by loneliness because her husband was never at home. Emilie hated to think that she might have been hiding the anguish of knowing that her husband was betraying her too.

Maman had wanted to send Emilie away to England in those last months, when she could no longer hide what was happening to her, but Emilie had clung to her, refusing to leave. They had been close; in those last two years even closer than mother and daughter usually were, just because they had both known their time together was going to be short. Emilie still missed her.

Her father's remarriage had been a shock of a different sort. Marie-Claude had worked on his newspaper; they had known each other for years, Emilie realised. Marie-Claude was in her early thirties, very French, sophisticated, elegant in that French way, understated and witty. Marie-Claude's clothes reflected Marie-Claude's mind. It would have been easier if she had been openly hostile—but Marie-Claude was far too clever for that.

She was very polite and gracious whenever she saw Emilie. She bought her new clothes, she suggested a change of hairstyle—as if they were going to be friends. But there was no warmth in her. As soon as she was pregnant with her first child she sent Emilie off to boarding-school. Her visits to her father's new home were always brief; after a week or so she would be sent off on some activity holiday—skiing in winter, horse-riding in summer. After leaving school she was despatched to a residential college in England, to take business studies. When she completed her two-year course Emilie began working for her grandfather at the paper-mill in Kent. She knew she would never live with her father again.

She had accepted it, yet there was always a sadness at the back of her mind. She tried to bury it by concentrating on her new life, on her grandfather and her job.

Emilie was learning the business by moving around the departments; she had spent some months on the most important process—production—moved on to a brief spell in packing and despatch, and was now working in sales.

She was at a very low level, of course. All she did was sit at a desk doing paperwork. Her grandfather didn't employ any women on the actual sales team; he didn't think it was a woman's job, travelling the roads across the country alone by car, staying at cheap hotels. He certainly wasn't prepared to let Emilie do it. She had to learn all about sales from processing orders as they came in from the salesmen and answering the phone, coping with enquiries.

She enjoyed dealing with people, she liked the other girls she worked with, and she was beginning to be very interested in their product, in the history of the paper-mill, in her mother's family. After a rather lonely period of her life she felt she had come home, she belonged here, and Sophie Grant and her mother were family too, as well as being the first people she had got to know here, except her grandfather. She would never want to hurt either of them, especially Sophie.

She frowned. Why was Grandpa so cynical about Aunt Rosa and Sophie? They seemed so fond of him.

Emilie hadn't seen Sophie since Saturday, since that party, in fact. When she did, she could hardly ask her if she was in love with Ambrose!

I'd better not mention him, in fact, she thought, getting dressed. It would be tactless to say much to Sophie about him. She might have been badly hurt when they broke up.

Why had they broken up, anyway? Had Ambrose ever been in love with Sophie?

She stopped brushing her hair, bit her lip, then glared at herself in the mirror. What's it got to do with you what happened? Stop thinking about him—he's twice your age, he probably has another woman now, a man

like him isn't going to be alone for long—I bet he's forgotten he ever met you!

She ran downstairs to breakfast at a quarter to eight,
and found her grandfather already at the table, in his
faintly old-fashioned dark suit, with a stiff red-striped
white shirt and maroon silk tie, eating toast and marmalade and drinking coffee, his normal weekday
breakfast.

He looked up and smiled, his eyes approving of her
crisp cream cotton blouse and dark grey pleated skirt,
of the way her sleek brown hair swirled around her face,
the brightness of her eyes and smile.

George Rendell had lived alone for years; loneliness
had been engrained in his mind, had got under his skin.
He had almost forgotten how it felt to live with someone
else, to have someone running up and down the stairs,
talking on the phone, watching television. He had forgotten what it was like to look across the breakfast-table
each morning and see another face, meet a warm smile.

Emilie had changed his life. He had wondered at first
if it would work for her to live with him, if he would
be irritated and bored having a young girl around all
day, but within a week it was as if she had always been
there.

More than that, he felt a strange new happiness welling
up inside him. He wasn't the type to show his feelings,
but the sun came out whenever he saw her come into a
room. She called out all his protective instincts—she was
young and small and helpless, and George would have
killed anyone who hurt her.

Emilie kissed him on the top of his head. 'Isn't it a
nice day?'

He looked at the window, saw the leafless trees in his
garden, the chilly sky. Almost Christmas—he hated

winter more each year. 'At least it isn't raining.' He watched her slide bread into the toaster, pour herself orange juice and coffee and sit down to eat opposite him.

'Everything OK for tonight?' he asked, and she nodded, spreading thick, chunky marmalade on her toast.

'We're having broccoli soup—at this time of year a hot soup is a good starter—then poached salmon in hollandaise sauce, which is light and simple, followed by a sweet omelette... I thought I'd fill it with hot purée of fruit, probably redcurrants or raspberries.'

She had learnt to cook from her mother, first, and one of the activity holidays forced upon her by her stepmother had been a summer at a *cordon bleu* cooking school on the Loire. Her grandfather had been astonished and delighted by this unexpected skill; he was used to eating dull food plainly cooked by his housekeepers, and he had eagerly begun giving dinner parties to show off Emilie's talent.

'Sounds delicious, mouth-watering,' he said fondly. 'Is Mary coming in to help you?'

'Oh, that's all arranged—there's no problem, Grandpa, don't worry. I'll make the soup in advance. The salmon is easy, it will only take me a quarter of an hour to cook it and make the sauce. The omelettes will take longer, but they aren't difficult. I shall cook them at the table on a spirit-stove—people always enjoy watching!'

'Watching other people work is always fun,' George grunted, smiling. He loved to watch her do anything; she endlessly fascinated him. 'I've never heard of omelettes filled with fruit.'

'It's really easy. I'll have prepared the fruit beforehand, it will be reheated in the microwave and brought to the table in a jug, so that I can pour it into the omelette just before I fold and serve it.'

'You're a marvel!' George Rendell said, and Emilie gave him a glowing look. Knowing he loved her made her feel she could do anything.

They drove to work at the paper-mill in Kent together, and that evening they drove home again, leaving on the dot of five o'clock. Her grandfather no longer worked the long hours he once had, she gathered. He had been a workaholic; now he preferred to be home with her.

It took them an hour to reach the house in Chelsea, and Emilie went straight into the kitchen. Their guests were not due for an hour and a half, which gave her just enough time to prepare most of the food before she went upstairs to dress for dinner.

The woman who came in every day to clean the house always helped with dinner parties. Emilie had left her instructions and Mary had already done some of the work—the vegetables were all prepared, the table laid, the ingredients ready.

Emilie rapidly made the broccoli soup and then puréed, separately, the raspberries and oranges she had decided on for the omelette-filling, then she went upstairs to shower and change. She couldn't make up her mind what to wear and wasted time putting on first one dress then another, hating herself in all of them. She wanted to look different. Older, more sophisticated. In the end she despairingly settled on a simple black dress her stepmother had bought her. Marie-Claude's taste was always perfect.

She did her hair and make-up and looked at herself in the mirror, and was startled by her reflection. The black dress certainly made her look different.

She dithered—should she wear it? Would it make Ambrose notice her, realise she wasn't the little girl he had seemed to think she was?

She looked again, making a face. Notice me? Not a chance. He was kind to me the other night because I was crying, but a man like him isn't interested in girls my age!

Should she change again, into something familiar? She looked at her watch and gave a cry of panic—there was no time! She had to hurry downstairs. Her grandfather met her at the foot of the stairs, his jaw dropping at the sight of her.

'Where did that dress come from? Bit old for you, isn't it?' His voice was dubious.

Her colour rose. 'Marie-Claude gave it to me,' she whispered.

'Who? Oh, your stepmother. Ah. French, is it?' Again that doubtful glance. 'Yes. Looks it.'

He hates it, she thought. If I rush I might have time to change; we can have dinner a few minutes late. But just then the doorbell went and the first of the guests arrived, and after that she had no chance to go and change.

They were all middle-aged or older, George Rendell's friends, kind to Emilie but way out of her age-group. She took their coats, with Mary hovering to take them away, poured them drinks, handed round plates of hors-d'oeuvres: sausages or prunes wrapped in crisp bacon, her own home-made cheese straws dipped in paprika, triangles of toast on which she had arranged caviare.

Ambrose was the last to arrive. At Emilie's first glimpse of him, her heart gave such a heavy thud that she felt almost sick.

'I'm sorry, I got caught in a traffic jam in Trafalgar Square,' he said as she opened the door to him, and then his eyes moved down over her and he frowned.

Shaken by that look, Emilie huskily asked, 'May I take your coat?' He hates my dress too, she thought, her heart sinking. Grandpa didn't like it, neither does Ambrose! Oh, why did I put it on?

Still staring, he shouldered out of the black cashmere, which was lined with dark red silk. Emilie reverently took it over her arm, unable to resist stroking it with one hand, thinking how soft and smooth it was—it must have cost a bomb!—and yet absorbing at the same time the fact that under the coat he was wearing a dark grey suit which was equally elegant and expensive. Made by the same tailor, no doubt; his clothes had an exclusive gloss. Her grandfather said that a man was judged by other men from how he dressed; Ambrose Kerr probably bought his clothes to impress his bank's clients. Did he always dress so formally? she wondered.

Tonight there was a gold watch-chain gleaming across his waistcoat, gold cufflinks in the cuffs of his white shirt, and he wore a dove-grey silk tie.

On any other man she would have thought the clothes stuffy and boring, but he made them sexy and exciting.

As if aware of her staring, he said, 'I came straight from work.' Then, abruptly, he said, 'You look different tonight—older, somehow. It's that dress.'

Tears prickled stupidly in her eyes, and she lowered them, gesturing to the open door nearby, from which came the sound of talking, laughter. 'Do go in,' she muttered. 'I must hang up your coat.'

As she turned stumblingly away Ambrose caught her shoulder to stop her, put a hand under her chin and lifted her face towards him, his grey eyes searching hers.

'You aren't upset, are you? The dress is very chic, and you're lovely in it. It's just that I had this idea of you from the other night—you were wearing a blue dress that made you look like Alice in Wonderland. Black makes you look much older, that's all.'

He hated her dress, he thought she was a little girl...
Alice in Wonderland! She broke away without a word and fled, taking his coat with her, and heard her grandfather greeting him behind her.

'Come and meet some people... What will you have to drink, Ambrose?'

It was a relief to have work to do, an excuse for not returning to the others yet. She went to the kitchen to reheat the broccoli soup, poured it into a tureen, and got Mary to take it to the dining-room.

Emilie put the vegetables on to cook, made the sauce to accompany the poached salmon, and slid the fish into the water, then she hurried through into the dining-room after setting the timer so that Mary would have a warning when the salmon was ready.

Mary had served the soup by the time Emilie took her seat; Ambrose was sitting opposite her.

'Your grandfather tells me you cooked the entire meal,' he said, his spoon poised.

Faces turned to smile at her. 'She's a wonderful cook,' one of the other guests, a frequent visitor, assured him.

'I've asked her to come and cook for me when I have dinner parties; she's wasted working at the mill,' another woman said. 'But she refuses to turn professional, says she's just an amateur. But I can't get any so-called professionals who can cook as well as Emilie.'

'It's just a hobby,' Emilie said, shyly pink.

Ambrose tasted the soup; everyone watched him, smiling.

He lowered his spoon. 'Delicious. They're right, you are good.'

Her blush deepened. Everyone laughed and began to eat, the tide of conversation rising along the table.

'If I invited you to cook for me, would you turn me down too?' he murmured, and she laughed but didn't answer.

Her grandfather spoke to him and Emilie was able to concentrate on her soup, her head lowered. She listened to everything they said, though, absorbing the sound of Ambrose's voice through every pore, memorising every intonation, the warm sound of his laughter when Grandpa told him a joke.

When she began cooking the omelettes at the table he insisted on helping her, adjusting the spirit-stove, holding the jug of fruit she would pour into the omelettes before serving.

Feeling his stare riveted on her made her very nervous, which was silly. She had cooked at the table before—made crêpes Suzette with Grand Marnier—but this time she was shaking a little and breathless, because Ambrose Kerr was standing beside her, watching her.

Somehow, though, she got through without making a mistake. Ambrose held out a warmed plate on to which she slid the finished omelette.

When he tasted the golden semicircle he sat with eyes half closed for a moment while the other guests all watched him, then said, 'Magnificent!' and everyone laughed.

'You are an amazing cook,' he told her over coffee. 'Your grandfather tells me you're working in the paper-mill. It seems a waste for someone who can cook as well as you can!'

Seriously, she said, 'Cooking is fun, but I love working in the mill far more. Our family have owned it for a century, you know, and it is a fascinating process, making paper.' She paused. 'Sorry, I mustn't bore you.'

'If you bored me I wouldn't be here,' he said, and Emilie drew a sharp, shaken breath. What did he mean by that?

Their eyes met across the table; her skin was burning, she was trembling. Was he flirting with her? If only she understood more about men!

'How is paper made?' Ambrose said, after a pause that seemed to last forever.

'I'm sure you already know!' Was he patronising her now? She prickled at the idea and he shot her an amused look, his mouth curling at one side.

'I have a hazy idea, but I've never studied the process in detail. I realise it comes from wood, of course.'

Emilie decided to take him at his word; if that bored him it would be his own fault! She told him how paper was made today, how it had been made in the past and how slight was the difference, merely a matter of more efficient machinery rather than a change in the actual process. Once she was over her intense awareness of him her eyes began to glow with the light of an enthusiasm close to passion.

That is how she would look in love, Ambrose thought, his eyes moving from her warm, softly full little mouth to her wide, bright blue eyes, roaming over her high cheekbones, her delicate temples, the fall of silky brown hair framing her face, and then going back to that mouth. It had passion and sweetness and sensitivity, only waiting for the right man to set fire to it.

After dinner George Rendell persuaded Emilie to play the piano for them; the guests all sat at one end of a

long, panelled room, the lights dimmed as if in an au-
ditorium, and Emilie sat at the piano at the other end.

'What are you going to play?' Ambrose asked, and
then insisted on glancing through the music-books she
produced. He picked a piece of Chopin she said she knew
and sat beside her while she played, turning the music
for her, leaning forward every so often to flip the page
over. Emilie was deeply conscious of him there, his strong
fingers moving just at the periphery of her sight, his gold
cufflinks glittering.

'You're good,' he said later, when she had finished
playing and everyone was talking again. 'Did you ever
think of doing that professionally?'

She shook her head, bright-eyed from his praise.

'Another hobby?' he teased.

'I'm not serious enough about either cooking or
playing the piano to do either of them professionally.
You need to be totally committed for that. I suppose I'm
too lazy.' Under her offhand tone Emilie felt guilty about
not having the sort of ambition and drive she knew she
ought to have. She had been given talents she wasn't
using; she could make a career with either cooking or
the piano, no doubt, if she worked at them, but at the
time when she should have been giving all of herself to
studying she had been too intent on her dying mother
to have the energy to spare, and after her mother finally
died Emilie had not felt she wanted to do anything at
all.

But she couldn't explain that to him; it was too personal, involved telling him too much, so she changed the
subject, asking him, 'What about you? Don't you have
any hobbies?'

He made a wry face. 'I paint, with a knife or my
hands—just splash oil-paints on in thick blobs. It helps

with aggressive feelings, I'm told. I'm not very good. It's more therapy than art.'

'It sounds fun to me. I haven't painted since I left school, and then we just did water-colours, very neat, pale water-colours. I'd like to try oil-painting, especially the way you just described.' She laughed, and said lightly, 'Maybe I need therapy!'

He didn't take her seriously. She couldn't need help of that kind, this wide-eyed girl barely out of childhood and spoiled by a doting grandfather! What problems could she have?

His voice very casual, he said, 'I usually paint at my place in the country. I have a house in the Cotswolds, with great views of the Malvern Hills—why don't you and your grandfather come for the weekend, and I'll show you what I laughingly call my technique? If you enjoy painting that way, you could start having professional lessons.'

Emilie hadn't expected that. Her breath caught, there was a beat of time before she could talk, then she huskily said, 'That would be wonderful, thank you.'

'Shall we check with your grandfather and see if he is free?' asked Ambrose, steering her over to where George Rendell was talking to some departing guests.

George was taken aback by the invitation. He had never been invited to Ambrose's country home before— their relationship was strictly a business one in London— but he accepted.

'Lovely part of the country, the Cotswolds,' he added. 'I'll look forward to seeing it again. I shan't be joining your painting class, though, Ambrose, not one for splashing paint around. I'll just relax by the fire and read the Sunday papers, I expect!'

Ambrose gravely said, 'You're coming for the weekend to relax, George. Do just whatever you like.' To Emilie he said, 'If it's cold, in winter, I paint in a conservatory—it gives all the light you need but it is warmer than being outside!'

'I don't mind cold weather,' she said.

'She doesn't feel the cold, lucky child,' said her grandfather, and Ambrose's eyes darkened.

He looked at her with sombre intensity. Child, he thought; she is a child, he's right. I'm out of my mind. What the hell do I think I'm going to do with her? I couldn't marry her, she's far too young. And if I seduce her, George will take a gun to me. Then his gaze drifted down to that soft, inviting pink mouth again. Come off it, you know what you'd like to do with her! he derisively told himself.

When Ambrose got home that evening he rang Gavin, who was in bed, but was immediately alert at the sound of the familiar voice.

'Ambrose? Anything wrong?'

'About the Rendell project,' Ambrose said curtly. 'I've decided to deal with that myself from now on. You can leave it entirely to me.'

Gavin's voice held suspicion, wariness. 'Why? Has something happened that I don't know about? A problem come up?'

Ambrose ignored the questions. 'You can draw up a new analysis of our manufacturing clients and their current positions.'

'Anyone could do that for you!' Gavin muttered. 'You had an analysis done only six months ago.'

'And now I want a new one, OK? Just drop the Rendell project, forget all about it.'

'You can't——' began Gavin, anger in his voice.

'Don't tell me what I can or can't do!'

Gavin audibly drew breath, shaken by the crack of Ambrose's voice. 'No, of course not, I wouldn't...didn't mean... Ambrose, I've run myself ragged to get them all to agree to your plans. Some of that board are old friends of his and needed a hell of a lot of persuading. Why are you taking me off the case?'

'That's my business. Just do what you're told, will you?'

Ambrose slammed the phone down, got into bed and sat up against his banked pillows staring at nothing, his face tense and pale.

A child, he reminded himself again. She was just a child. It was crazy. He couldn't. Shouldn't. She still had so much to learn about life, about herself, about men—especially men like him. She was gentle, sweet, innocent... He had no right to go anywhere near her.

He had years of experience behind him, in every sense of the word. Other women had taught him what he knew about her sex, not all of them very nice women, some of them not women he would even want her to meet.

She was a sheet of pure white paper on which life had not yet written a word. Heat burned deep inside him, though, at the thought of teaching her, being the first. There was something about that purity, that innocence, that he found exciting.

She might be sexually unawakened, but all his male instincts told him there was passion waiting inside her to be kindled. That full, soft mouth invited exploration.

By someone her own age, he told himself scathingly, not someone like me!

There were parts of his life he hated to remember, a darkness he sometimes met in his nightmares and which made him wake up in sweating misery. She couldn't even begin to imagine what his life had been like; did he have any right to let that darkness touch her, even remotely?

Her grandfather would certainly object; he didn't know Ambrose very well. Ambrose had made sure that nobody knew anything about his origins. His life had begun when he arrived in London, when he was twenty, much the age of this girl.

He had suppressed his background, buried the darkness where nobody could ever find it, but George Rendell was no fool. He would have no more luck in tracing Ambrose to his roots than anyone else had done during the past fifteen years, that distant past was too well hidden, but he would still have a good idea that Ambrose wasn't a suitable man to be in his granddaughter's life.

He's right, too, thought Ambrose. I should stop this now. Before someone gets hurt. I'd hate to hurt her. I'd hate myself if I did. If I seduce her, sooner or later she'll get hurt, when it's all over.

His love affairs had never lasted long. There was no room for a full-time commitment in his life; he was too busy, his sex drive had to fit in with his over-busy schedule and women always wanted more than he could give them. They wanted stability, marriage, children.

He had always just wanted sex.

No, he couldn't do it; an innocent like that needed someone of her own generation, a boy whose experience matched her own.

Sholto Cory? mocked a cold, inner voice—and, at the very idea of them together, jealousy hit him like an arrow in the dark. He shuddered. No, he's too young; he wouldn't appreciate her mixture of unaware sensuality and shining innocence the way an older man would. He would rush at her greedily and bruise that sweetness.

A girl like her needed gentler handling: patience, a slow introduction to the pleasure of sex, not to be grabbed and...

He groaned, flinging an arm across his face. Who was he kidding? The truth was, he couldn't bear the idea of Sholto laying a hand on her. He wanted her for himself.

He called a florist next morning and sent Emilie roses; he wanted white ones but the girl ruefully assured him she could only manage either red or pale pink.

'Pink, then,' Ambrose said. 'Two dozen.'

They arrived while Emilie was at work, and Mary put them into green glass vases for her and arranged them in the sitting-room.

'That's nice of him,' her grandfather said, staring at them. 'He certainly knows how to make a gesture.'

'Aren't they beautiful?' Emilie said dreamily, touching a rose with gentle fingers. The petals were like cool velvet, their colour the delicate pale pink of mother-of-pearl.

The doorbell rang, Mary went to answer it; they heard her talking and then a male voice replying.

'Sholto!' Emilie said, and George Rendell grimaced.

'That young man... What is he doing here at this hour? Have you asked him to dinner?'

'No, I wouldn't, without asking you first. You know that!'

'If he stays long, we shall have to ask him, I suppose!' George muttered, and stamped off to get himself a drink. He liked Sholto well enough, but the dinner party had used up all his hospitable feelings; he had been looking forward to an evening spent quietly at home with just Emilie for company.

Sholto came in, bringing a rush of cold air with him, and gave her a hopeful look. 'Hi, I thought you might like to come and see a film—there's a terrific thriller on at the moment.'

She sighed, wishing he hadn't come. She was trying to avoid him at the moment; she still hadn't got over that proposal during Ambrose Kerr's Christmas party. Sholto had been far too insistent; he had scared her off.

'I'm sorry, Sholto, I'm too tired tonight. I had a lot to do at work today.'

'Oh, come on, Em,' he said, his mouth sulky.

She had given in before when he looked like that, because she had felt guilty about refusing, but not this time. She firmly shook her head.

'I want to get an early night; I have another busy day tomorrow.'

As she turned away her sleeve caught a small card which had been resting against one of the vases of roses; it fluttered to the ground and Sholto bent to pick it up.

Before she could stop him he had read it. He looked at the roses, scowling. 'He sent you those? How many are there? There must be a couple of dozen... Pink roses in December? They must have cost an arm and a leg! Why did he send them? What the hell is going on, Emilie?'

CHAPTER THREE

EMILIE knew Ambrose was going to be at the board-meeting on Thursday morning at ten-thirty. She kept her eye on her watch and at about ten-twenty began her weekly job of first pruning and tidying up, then watering the plants on the windowsill in the office, while she threw an occasional casual glance out of the window at the car-park below. Other directors arrived, parked, went into the office block to make their way up to the board-room, but Ambrose was late.

Just after half-past ten, a silvery-blue Rolls drew up and slid silently into a parking place; then his long legs emerged, followed by his lean, hard body. He was wearing a camel-hair coat today; as he moved it swung open, revealing one of those elegantly tailored dark city suits, a red-striped shirt, a dark red silk tie.

He got a black leather briefcase out of the back of the limousine, locked the Rolls, turned and began to walk, then threw a rapid look upwards, over the windows of the building, as if he could feel her presence.

Emilie shot back from her window so fast that she hit her thigh on her desk.

'Ouch!' She dropped her watering-can, shedding water all over the carpet, and lifted her skirt to scrutinise the rapidly darkening bruise on her upper leg.

There were two other girls in the room, working at word-processors. They looked up at her cry of pain.

'That looks nasty,' Jennifer, a small, dark girl of her own age said.

The older girl, Karen, was always quick with advice. She told Emilie, 'You should rub it, to disperse the blood; it helps.'

Emilie rubbed her thigh, grimacing, then picked up the watering-can, looking ruefully at the damp stain on the carpet.

'You'd better get a cloth from the cleaners' cupboard and mop that up,' Karen told her.

Emilie emptied the watering-can down a sink in the cupboard-like room on that corridor where the cleaners kept their various pieces of equipment, and hunted for a cloth to use on the carpet.

The board-room was just a few doors away. She could hear the low buzz of voices. She had sat in on one board-meeting, months ago, but it had been short and dull. She didn't remember Ambrose being present; she was sure she would have noticed him if he had been there.

The bruise on her leg still ached; she pulled up her skirt again to squint down at it, frowning. It showed black and blue against the creamy smooth flesh of her thigh. What did you put on bruises? Witch-hazel? Something soothing—a cream?

'How did you do that?' a deep voice asked, and she started, flicking a look at the door.

Ambrose's eyes were fixed on her bared thigh, on the deep lace of her white slip, the tiny, silky white panties under that.

She hurriedly dropped her skirt.

Ambrose watched the hot pink flow up her face, the widening of those blue eyes.

'Oh...hello...' she stammered, her lips parting in a breathless gasp. 'Thank you for the roses, they were lovely,' she said, wishing he wouldn't stare like that.

He shrugged. 'Glad you liked them. You didn't say how you got the bruise.'

'Bumped myself on my desk,' she said, very flushed.

'You should be more careful; you have the sort of skin that bruises easily.'

The sort of skin that made a man want to touch it, taste it, he thought. When he first saw her, at his Christmas party, he hadn't thought she was pretty, let alone beautiful, but every time he had seen her since, the impression she made got deeper, stronger.

But she's too damn young! he told himself impatiently. Don't even think about it. But he kept remembering that smooth, slim thigh, the delicate silky panties, the lace through which he had caught a glimpse of curly dark hair. Heat smouldered inside him.

'Were you looking for the board-room?' she asked, wondering what he was thinking—why was he scowling like that? Had she offended him somehow? 'It's just down the corridor; they'll be waiting for you.'

'Let them,' he said with cool arrogance, as if none of the other men on the board had anything better to do than wait for him, and perhaps some of them would agree with him. They were certainly prepared to wait without complaint, at least to him. Ambrose Kerr was a very powerful man, and it wasn't just his money that impressed other men. His personality was impressive, formidable.

He frightens me, Emilie thought, her pulses going haywire.

He looked at her through his dark lashes, his eyes gleaming. 'I saw you as I was walking past, so I came in to say how much I enjoyed the meal you cooked for us the other night.'

'Oh... good...' was all she could manage in reply. The room was so tiny, and he dominated the cramped space, imposed his physical presence on her. She felt a claustrophobic tightness in her throat, in her blood. If he came any nearer, if he touched her, even with a fingertip, she felt she would scream, her awareness of him was so intense.

Huskily, she said, 'Grandpa will wonder where you are.'

He smiled crookedly. 'Well, I mustn't keep your grandfather waiting, must I?'

He turned on his heel and vanished.

She sagged, closing her eyes. Behind her ribcage her heart clashed like cymbals, the sound seeming to echo through her blood.

Moving like a zombie, she found a cloth and went back to the office to mop up the floor, washed her hands, then sat down at her desk again to try and concentrate on work. It wasn't easy. Her mind kept wandering back to Ambrose. She wished she understood him better, could read that strong, controlled face of his more easily.

But that was just what he didn't want, wasn't it? Ambrose preferred to keep his secrets.

There was a sudden outburst of shouting from the board-room and all of the girls looked up, startled.

'Sounds like World War III just broke out. I wonder what's going on in there?' Karen said. 'Is something up, Emilie?'

'Not that I know of.' Emilie frowned. Her grandfather had said this morning that the board-meeting wouldn't last long; there was nothing important on the agenda.

The shouting got louder; they couldn't distinguish the words but the anger in the voices was unmistakable.

Emilie picked out Grandpa's voice, louder than anyone else's.

'I'd like to be a fly on the wall in there!' Jennifer said, giggling.

'Get on with your work,' Karen scolded. Almost thirty, and married, she had worked there longest and was in charge of the office. She treated the younger girls as if they were children sometimes, but she had a maternal streak and could be very kind.

At one o'clock, Karen and Jennifer went off to lunch. Someone always had to stay behind to man the office during the lunch-break. Today it was Emilie's turn. She answered the phone, worked at her computer, but her mind was preoccupied with Ambrose and the board-meeting, which still hadn't ended.

It was almost two o'clock when she heard the directors emerging. They walked past to the lift, a small crowd of men in suits, carrying briefcases, talking to each other; she caught snatches of sentences.

'Felt very bad about it... But that's life. Nothing stays the same, everything changes.'

'Tough character, Ambrose...'

'But knows what he's doing.'

'Oh, absolutely. I'm very fond of the old man, you know that, known him for years, great respect for him, but there's no denying he's well past his sell-by date; the firm needs someone with new ideas, new direction.'

'This is business, after all.'

'Well, there you have it! You can see the bank's point of view. Have to protect their investment.'

'That's the bottom line. It's ultimately the investors who count. The bank uses their money, they expect a good return. Have to protect jobs, too, don't forget.'

'Quite. There's always a risk of bankruptcy if the rot isn't stopped soon enough, and then the men would blame us. Hard decision to make, though. Glad I'm not in Ambrose's shoes. I need a drink—how about stopping at the pub on our way back, Don?'

Emilie sat listening, feeling cold. What were they talking about? What had been happening at that board-meeting?

Karen and Jennifer came back from lunch a moment or two later, and she was free to leave the office. She didn't tell the others what she had heard, and she wasn't hungry now; she didn't want lunch. She walked quietly down to the board-room door. It stood ajar; inside the narrow, rectangular room she saw Ambrose, his back to her, his black head lit by wintry sunlight which gave it a frosty gleam.

Her grandfather was sitting at the long board-room table, half hidden by Ambrose, his face in profile.

'How long have you been planning this?' he was asking in a hoarse voice. 'My God, you are a bastard, aren't you? Sweet as honey to my face, making out that we were the best of friends, and all the time you had a knife behind your back.'

Emilie stiffened, holding her breath.

'No, George,' Ambrose said quietly. 'Please don't make this personal; it isn't. I have the highest respect for you. I know you've given your life to this company and you really care about your work-force; that's why I hoped you'd see this change as being for the good of everyone who works here. It's business, George; nothing personal. You'll still own a big piece of the company, you'll still be on the board.'

'Without any power!'

'You'll still be there, though. You aren't just being kicked out.'

'Don't try to wrap it up! I've been given six months' notice!'

Emilie felt as if she had been punched in the stomach. She wanted to yell; instinctively she put her hand over her mouth, to silence herself. She didn't want them to know she was there; they would stop talking like this if they saw her, and she wanted to know exactly what was going on.

Had Grandpa lost the firm? But how? It was their firm, their family had built it up, her grandfather had run it for years, was a major shareholder—how could anyone take it away from them?

Ambrose sighed. 'George, you are way past the usual retirement age! You know very well you should have retired long ago.'

Furiously, George Rendell shouted at him, 'I don't want to retire. I enjoy my work. Who the hell are you, anyway, to dictate to me when I should stop work? You've cheated me...'

Emilie bit down on her knuckles. What exactly had Ambrose done?

'George, I haven't done anything of the kind!'

'You've sold my firm to that bastard Wingate!'

She knew that name; he was one of their main rivals, of a big Scottish firm who competed with them for markets. She had only heard of Ewan Wingate, she had never met him, but she knew her grandfather didn't like him. Their feud was of such long standing that the original quarrel had been lost in the mists of time, but they had kept it up for most of their working lives.

Ambrose sounded faintly impatient now. 'It wasn't mine to sell, George. I don't own any shares in your company.'

'Don't pretend you didn't engineer the whole deal. This didn't just happen! It was one of your carefully worked-out take-overs. I know your reputation, Kerr!'

Ambrose was silent. Emilie stared at the long, elegant line of his back, the tension in the muscles under that smooth suit.

Shock made her chill and sick.

'You betrayed me!' Grandpa said thickly, and the words were an echo of what she had been thinking. 'I'm not some turnip from the back of beyond. I know how you operate. You secretly talked shareholders into selling their shares to Wingate, you persuaded the board to vote me out as chairman and him into my job! I've lost control, and there's nothing I can do about it; I have to leave my own firm, retire when I'm not ready for it.'

'I'm sorry, but the bank lent you a very considerable sum, George. We hoped it would raise production, improve cash-flow, but that hasn't happened, has it?'

'Admittedly, we've had problems. We've had a bad recession to cope with, remember. But we're pulling out of it now. Our productivity has gone up, and when the buyers come back we'll be ready for them.'

Ambrose said curtly, 'Meanwhile your cash-flow has become a trickle, and you aren't paying back the loan, just the interest.'

'That's how you make your money, isn't it?' George Rendell said bitingly. 'You lend out money at exorbitant interest-rates! Oh, yes, and if someone can't pay, you foreclose on them! You can't lose. If we pay you back you get that monstrous rate of interest; if we can't pay, you take the firm away or fix up a deal with one of your other clients. It wouldn't surprise me to find out that you had this scheme in mind when I first approached you for money.'

'Don't be ridiculous!' snapped Ambrose. 'You're our client too. We want you to make money. But the accounts make depressing reading. We're a bank, George, not a charity. We have to safeguard our clients' money.'

'So you sold me out.'

Emilie couldn't bear the bleakness in her grandfather's voice. She moved impulsively; both men heard her. Grandpa stood up, his face changing. Ambrose swung round.

His grey eyes flashed over her pale face, searching her expression.

She looked at him with angry bitterness, walked past him without a word and went to her grandfather, put her arms around him, leant her head against his shoulder.

'Oh, Grandpa, I'm so sorry.'

He looked at her sharply. 'You know? Did he tell you? How long have you known?'

'I've been listening at the door,' she confessed, hearing the suspicion under his tone and hating to see distrust in his face.

'Oh, I see,' he said, holding her close, sighing with a sort of sick relief. 'I was afraid... Never mind...'

She looked up at him. 'Afraid of what?'

'That you might be in on it,' he said.

She turned even paler. 'You thought I...? You can't have thought I would do that to you?'

'No, of course you wouldn't, I'm sorry,' he said. 'Emilie... we've lost the mill, they've taken it away from us.'

She looked at him helplessly, wishing there was something she could say to help him, something she could do. Tears glittered in her blue eyes. 'But how, Grandpa? I don't understand what's happened.'

He talked in a gritty way, his teeth barely parting. He was so pale; she was worried by the look of him. 'I owed them a lot of money; some of my shares were put up as collateral. The bank can now take possession of them. And a lot of other shares have changed hands—Wingate had bought a big chunk of shares today without my being aware of what was going on.' His face and voice were charged with bitterness. 'My "friends" on the board . . . Some of them sold out to Wingate, others didn't sell but voted with Kerr and his gang, forcing me off the board, putting Wingate on to it.'

She looked accusingly at Ambrose.

'I'm trying to save your firm, Emilie,' he said in a voice which was deep and harsh. 'It is in a very bad way. If your grandfather is honest, he'll admit that. The firm has been making plenty of product but isn't selling enough. Unless something is done—and soon—the mill may have to shut down.'

'He's a smooth liar, Emilie, don't believe a word he says!' George Rendell struggled to his feet, his knuckles turning white as he clutched the desk. She put an arm round his waist to support him, and he leaned on her so heavily that she almost buckled under his weight. 'Let's go home,' he added in a weary way. 'I can't take any more.'

Ambrose said curtly, 'George, I'm sorry you're taking it so badly, but——'

'Leave him alone!' Emilie interrupted him with fury. 'Come on, Grandpa, I'll take you home.'

They began to walk towards the lift, but George was breathing badly; they had to keep stopping.

Emilie was angrily aware of Ambrose walking just behind them. The lift doors were open; she guided her grandfather through them and Ambrose joined them. George and Emilie ignored him as the lift went down, George Rendell leaning on the wall and breathing thickly.

Emilie was increasingly worried about him. He seemed to have aged ten years in one morning.

As they walked out of the lift he swayed and almost fell over, taking Emilie with him. Ambrose was there instantly, his powerful body supporting her, taking over, pushing her aside and half carrying the old man towards the silvery-blue Rolls-Royce.

'I'm going home in my own car!' George Rendell growled thickly, trying to push Ambrose away.

'You're in no condition to drive.'

'I'll drive,' Emilie said coldly.

'You may need help with him. If anything happened... If there was an emergency on the way...'

'I can deal with any emergency,' she insisted. 'Leave us alone. We don't want your help.'

George Rendell pushed him away, straightening. 'I'm not on my last legs yet!' He turned to their own car, opened the passenger door, struggled, half fell into the seat, and slammed the door shut behind him.

Emilie went round to get behind the wheel, but Ambrose caught her wrist and held her back.

His grey eyes glittered. 'Don't judge me without letting me tell you my side of the story.'

She gave him a bitter, reproachful stare. 'You're taking my family firm away from us. What more do I need to know?'

'Emilie, it's just a management reshuffle—your family still owns a large part of the company. The only change is that your grandfather won't be running it any more.'

'All that is just words. The fact is, you've taken our firm and handed it to the man my grandfather hates most in the world. He and Ewan Wingate have had a feud for years. Now Wingate has got hold of our mill. All because of you.' She looked up at him with hatred. 'Now get your hand off me. I hope I never set eyes on you again.'

Ambrose let his hand drop, didn't answer her—just stood there like a figure carved in stone.

Emilie got into the car. As she started the engine Ambrose seemed to come out of his trance; he leapt at the car as if to stop it, said something she didn't catch. She drove away without so much as a glance, almost running him over.

When they got home she put her grandfather to bed. He lay there, his hands clenched on the quilt covering him, his face grey, his breathing bad.

'Try to rest,' Emilie said, biting her lip, then she went downstairs and called their family doctor, who came at once.

After examining George, he joined her downstairs, his face grave. 'He's an old man, Emilie; and I gather he's had a severe shock. But his heart is quite strong, although his blood-pressure isn't really satisfactory. Keep him in bed, don't let him excite himself, try to keep him calm; just a little light food, no alcohol, none of those cigars he loves to smoke. I'll call and see him tomorrow.'

'He seems so old suddenly,' she whispered.

The doctor gave her a kind smile. 'He is old, my dear. But he is basically in good health; don't worry. With love and care he will soon be back to normal.'

She barely slept that night. She was too edgy; worrying about her grandfather, worrying about the paper-mill, brooding over the way Ambrose had betrayed them.

In the morning she let her grandfather sleep while she went downstairs to make his breakfast. She had just put on the coffee when the doorbell rang.

The doctor had promised to come that morning. Emilie hurried to the front door, but as she opened it she caught sight of Ambrose outside and at once tried to slam the door shut again.

He put his powerful body into the opening, forcing the door back.

'Go away—if you had an ounce of decency, you wouldn't show your face around here.'

'How's your grandfather?' he answered coolly, pushing his way inside the house.

She couldn't stop him, she wasn't strong enough, but she looked at him with contempt.

'Don't pretend you care!'

'I do, Emilie,' he insisted in a low voice, those black brows of his dragging together.

Bitterly she said, 'Only because you're hoping you've managed to kill him, so that you can buy up the rest of his shares!'

His eyes glittered fiercely. 'I haven't any personal interest in all this—how many times do I have to tell you? I won't be buying any shares in your company. I am acting solely in the interests of my investors, in protecting money I lent your grandfather. I wish it wasn't necessary.'

She laughed disbelief, saw his face tighten even more and felt an odd satisfaction at having made him angry. Ambrose was used to people jumping to attention when he spoke, agreeing with everything he said, believing him implicitly, or pretending to. Well, he wouldn't get that from her.

'Listen,' he said through his teeth. 'Whatever you think of me, if you love your grandfather you'll persuade him to accept what's happened, and make the best of the new situation.'

'Get him to go quietly, you mean?' she mocked, and a dark red crept up his face.

'No, I did not mean that!' he snarled, making her jump.

'Don't you shout at me!' She wasn't letting him see he scared her, even though he did.

He drew in a long, audible breath, visibly fighting to control his temper.

'Look, I'm trying to persuade you not to encourage him to cut his nose off to spite his face. The bank still holds those shares of his as collateral for the loan. I won't dispose of them to anyone else and——'

'You mean, he could still get the mill back?' she interrupted, with a leap of hope.

'He is too old to run the mill, Emilie!' Ambrose bit out impatiently.

She tensed at the lash of his voice.

'You're shouting again!'

'Then don't make me angry!' he muttered, staring down at her and running his hand through his hair in a gesture of baffled impatience. 'Try to understand what I'm saying to you. Stop seeing me as some sort of cardboard villain in a pantomime. I want to reach a compromise, OK?'

'What do you mean, compromise?' she asked warily.

'Your grandfather hasn't got the drive, the energy required to get the company back on the right track. He can only go on from day to day in the same old way. That simply isn't enough these days. But that doesn't mean he couldn't continue to be on the board, continue to work there as an adviser, still have a strong voice in the firm.'

He made it all sound far too sensible, too convincing. Emilie hated him for that. It was easier to believe that he had betrayed Grandpa, had only unworthy motives for what he had done. She didn't want him to persuade her to see it his way.

Angrily, she told him, 'He wouldn't take orders from someone else!'

Ambrose was quick to insist, 'He wouldn't have to take orders. He would still have his own office, and a secretary. He wouldn't be there to work for someone else, just to advise. Wingate doesn't intend to take over personally; he is putting a good manager in there. A young man, but experienced and full of ideas—in fact, your grandfather knows him. He used to work for him at one time before he moved on to a place in the Midlands, and later to work for Wingate. Stephen Hawdry—do you know him?'

She shook her head, but the name was vaguely familiar; she thought her grandfather had mentioned it at some time.

'He has a lot of respect for your grandfather; he'll try to make this arrangement work. He'll listen to George, ask his advice.' Ambrose looked down into her troubled blue eyes. 'Emilie, persuade him to give Hawdry a chance; it will be for his own good if you do.'

'Not to mention for yours!' she said bitterly. 'It will ease your conscience, what little you have! And make it easier for you to get on with your next coup and forget about us.'

'That isn't true!' he snapped back. 'For God's sake, Emilie...' He stopped short, drew a long breath, his grey eyes brooding on her. 'Look, persuade him to talk to

me. Come down to the Cotswolds as we arranged; if I
have all weekend I may manage to get through to him.'

She bit her lip. If Grandpa could still go to the mill
every day, was still on the board, he would have something to keep him going. She was desperately afraid that
losing all contact with the firm might make him lose his
will to live.

Ambrose was watching her intently. 'Will you do that,
Emilie?'

'I'll think about it,' she grudgingly agreed. 'Now, will
you please leave before he hears your voice and comes
down to find out what's going on? I don't want him
getting upset again.'

For a minute she thought he wasn't going; he stood
there, watching her, making her intensely aware of him,
of the physical power of his body, of the glittering,
brooding eyes.

'I'm sorry this has had to happen,' he said abruptly.

Ambrose saw that look in her face, and knew he wasn't
getting through to her. She was too young to know the
meaning of the word compromise, he thought, frowning.
Too passionate, as well. He looked at her soft, full
mouth, at the way anger was making her breath fast,
her breasts rising and falling with each sharp intake of
air. If she looked like that when she was merely angry,
how would she look in the act of love? he thought, and
his own body clenched in sudden, piercing excitement.
He pulled himself up. Gritted his teeth. Stop it! he told
himself. She's half your age and as innocent as a child.
You've no business even thinking about her like that; if
she knew she would be horrified, scared stiff.

He swallowed and said thickly, 'Don't let your anger
with me stop you doing the right thing. I'm not asking
you to do this for me—I'm asking you to do it for your

grandfather, Emilie. I'll ring you tonight to find out what you decided to do.'

Her blue eyes hostile, she met his stare head-on, still without speaking. Ambrose's mouth compressed. He turned and went out, and Emilie slammed the door behind him.

CHAPTER FOUR

EMILIE knew she was going to talk to her grandfather, of course. She might resent what Ambrose had said, but she couldn't deny he made sense. Only getting back to work at the mill and re-establishing the habits of his whole life could help her grandfather avoid some sort of breakdown.

George Rendell was furious when she first broached the subject. He erupted in a rage, glaring at her.

'Spend the weekend with him? I never want to set eyes on him again!'

'I understand how you feel, Grandpa, but——'

'No!' he shouted. 'I don't want to hear another word on the subject.'

Emilie held his hand and looked pleadingly at him. 'Sooner or later you're going to have to talk to him, if you want to have a say in what happens to the company in future.'

'He's sold it to Wingate. I am not talking to Wingate.'

'Grandpa——'

'And if I did, it would be useless. I know that old buzzard. He'll never let me have any power or influence in the company again. He has always wanted it, and now he's got it.' George Rendell ground his teeth, darkly flushed. 'And damn Ambrose Kerr to hell—it's his doing, and I won't forget it.'

'Mr Wingate isn't going to be involved in the actual running of the mill; he's putting in a manager, someone you know.' She told him everything Ambrose had told her, and her grandfather brightened.

'Stephen? He's a good boy. But manager? I don't know if he's up to that.'

'That's why Ambrose thinks they'll still need you. Please at least discuss it with him, Grandpa.'

'I am not discussing anything with Kerr,' George Rendell growled.

Emilie wasn't deflected; she gently repeated the same thing over and over again, in different ways, until he stopped shouting and groaned.

'Water dripping on a stone! That's your technique. Oh, very well, I'll spend the weekend there, and I'll talk to him, but I'm not promising to agree with a word he says, and I still think he's a treacherous swine.'

'So do I, but we can't beat him, Grandpa, so we're going to have to do a deal with him, aren't we?'

'Damn him,' George Rendell said, but the very fact that he had stopped arguing was a hopeful sign. He even looked better—as the doctor said to her, smiling his satisfaction.

'Rest and quiet—I told you it would do the trick.'

Ambrose's house in the Cotswold Hills was Georgian, built of a creamy golden stone and set in extensive, old-established gardens, surrounded by trees, mostly leafless now in the run-up to Christmas, yet still beautiful, the slender silver birch shining beside beech and chestnut, and here and there a magnificent oak or a great elm. Behind them stood a high wall of stone from a local quarry: grey stone, blueish flint, with a band of red brick running along the top in a Greek key pattern. It could only be glimpsed through the trees but it gave protection to the garden within it, a calm shelter from wind.

'I wonder who else he has invited?' her grandfather murmured as they drove through the open gate with its classic stone pillars on either side, under a tunnel of lime-trees, to emerge into wintry sunlight and catch a first glimpse of the perfect proportions of the house.

Emilie gave him a horrified look. 'Will there be other people there?'

'He won't just have invited us! I only hope to God he hasn't invited that rat Wingate. I wouldn't put it past him.'

Her heart sank. Ambrose's friends were bound to be banking people, way out of her own age-group: men who talked about money day and night, women in designer clothes who would look at her as if wondering what on earth she was doing here, raising their perfectly pencilled eyebrows in disbelief.

As their car drew up on the gravel outside the house, Ambrose appeared under the cream stone portico and her heart leapt like a stranded salmon trying to fight its way upstream against the current.

He came to open her door; his hand slid under her elbow as he helped her out and that light touch made her breathless, which, in turn, made her angry, because he could still affect her like that in spite of her contempt for his treachery, her bitterness because he had made her think he liked her, when all the time he had been plotting betrayal.

'Where do you want me to park the car?' George Rendell said, in curt, unfriendly tones, through the driver's window.

'If you drive through that entrance over there,' Ambrose said, 'you'll find yourself in a stableyard; there are two garages on the left. Park in either. But let's get your luggage out first.'

A short, stocky, bald man in a dark suit had joined them from the house; he and Ambrose got the luggage out of the car.

'Which is yours?' Ambrose asked Emilie, and she pointed to a dark brown leather case.

'This is Henry,' Ambrose told her. 'He'll take the cases to your rooms, and if you need anything while you're staying here you just ask him, or, if he isn't around, dial seven on the internal phone and you'll get either Henry or his wife, Susan.'

The man in the dark suit smiled at her, picked up both cases and vanished back into the house, while George Rendell drove off, negotiated the wide gateway between high stone walls, and disappeared.

Ambrose looked down at Emilie, his grey eyes flicking over her heathery tweed suit and the pale lavender sweater she wore under it.

'That colour suits you.'

Her colour high, she said stiffly, 'Thank you.' He needn't think he was getting round her that easily!

'Did you bring any jeans or trousers?'

'Jeans,' she admitted. 'Why?'

'I remember you said you rode with Sholto Cory in the forest. I've got a few horses here, if you'd like to ride.'

'Is anyone else staying here?'

He gave her a quick, hard look. 'No, you and your grandfather are the only guests, I'm afraid. Were you hoping to see someone else here?' Before she could answer he added curtly, 'Cory?'

'No. I knew he wasn't coming—I saw him on Wednesday.'

His eyes had a hard glitter. 'You're still dating him?'

'It wasn't a date—he came to the house to talk to me.'

'But you're still seeing him?' he bit out.

Sholto was still trying to apologise for having upset her at Ambrose's party; he realised it had made her very wary of him. 'I had too much to drink, I lost my head,' he had pleaded, looking like a little boy, and she had forgiven him—how could she help it? She was fond of Sholto. But she had refused to go out with him again; she didn't want him trying to persuade her to change her mind and get engaged.

'We're friends,' she said shortly.

Ambrose's brows met. 'He wants to be rather more to you than that, though, doesn't he? You shouldn't encourage him by seeing him.'

'I'm not discussing my private life with you!' she snapped.

'Maybe you want to encourage him?' he bit out, his grey eyes flashing.

'Maybe I do!' she retorted, lifting her chin defiantly. 'That's no business of yours.' She met his angry stare, her nerves prickling. He had no right to give her advice or interfere in her life, and he could stop looking at her as if he might slap her any minute.

It was a relief, all the same, to see her grandfather walking back through the gateway of the stableyard towards them.

Ambrose turned away from her to give her grandfather a forced, tight smile. 'Parked your car OK, George? Good. Come in and have a hot drink—you must need it after driving all the way from London.'

'The whole country is being strangled with traffic; there are too many damn cars on the roads!' George said gruffly, following him into the house. His upbringing made him feel he must be polite to his host,

but every hair on his head seemed to bristle every time
he spoke to Ambrose.

He had liked the man, now he hated him, and he was
too direct and blunt a man to hide his feelings.

Emilie walked into the house and stopped dead, blue
eyes wide, taking in golden oak panelling, deep-sunk
stone floors spread with old Axminster rugs, the faded
but still lovely eighteenth-century tapestries, showing
scenes of hunting and country pursuits.

There were flowers everywhere: bowls of dark red and
yellow chrysanthemums standing on old carved chests,
on deep window-seats, on tables, the smoky winter scent
of the flowers mingling with the smell of beeswax and
lavender and wood-smoke from the log fire in the great
stone fireplace.

'What a magnificent house!' George Rendell said,
startled into genuine admiration. 'How long have you
had it?'

'A few years,' Ambrose said curtly. 'Ah, here's the
coffee.'

George Rendell gave him a sharp look, took the hint
and asked him no more personal questions.

What was his background? wondered Emilie as they
were served their coffee. He kept trying to ask her personal questions, but he grew edgy whenever anyone tried
to ask him questions—what had he got to hide?

It was rare, these days, for someone to rise to the top
in his profession, make a private fortune, live like a
modern prince, without the media making his background public knowledge. How did Ambrose manage
it? It wasn't as if the Press weren't interested in him. He
was always appearing in the gossip-columns and the
financial pages of newspapers. He was rich, good-
looking and single—that made him fascinating to the

Press, who were always writing about him. They had tried to dig up his past, Sholto said, but had failed.

She watched his hard profile through her lashes, pondering the enigma that was Ambrose. Where was his family? Where did he come from?

Half an hour later, Ambrose took them to their rooms, which were next door to each other, with views of the winter-locked gardens and beyond that the countryside, the blue haze of the Malvern Hills in the background.

'Lunch is in an hour,' Ambrose told them. 'You'll probably want to settle in before that. I'll see you downstairs when you're ready.'

Left alone, Emilie unpacked, then wandered around, loving the French Empire style in which her room had been furnished. She was half-afraid to touch anything, the furniture was so exquisite.

The walls were papered in green-striped paper with gold laurel wreaths scattered here and there. There was a gondola-style bed made of gleaming walnut, with a dark green and gold canopy overhead and a green and gold damask bedcover.

The material was echoed in matching curtains at the window, with swags of gold-fringed damask along the top, and on each side of the bed were small cabinets on which stood green-shaded lamps on sculpted bronze stands. There was a pale green carpet, a delicate little dressing-table with gilded legs, two chests of drawers in the same style, on top of which stood a porcelain shepherd and shepherdess, each sitting under an apple-tree with their lambs beside them. The clothes of the figures were liberally sprinkled with tiny pale blue flowers. When she carefully lifted one and looked underneath, she found the crossed blue swords of

Meissen painted on the bottom. Hurriedly she put it down. It was probably worth a fortune!

Emilie had never seen anything so pretty in her life as that room. Had Ambrose furnished it himself? Or had he simply got an interior designer to come along and design the room for him, find all these lovely pieces of furniture, pick the fabrics and wallpaper?

Men weren't usually that interested in the way a house looked, were they? But Ambrose was a painter...even if only an amateur...

What do I know about men, though? she thought wryly, sighing. And especially about him! All I know about him is what Sholto has told me, and Sholto doesn't really know him at all, has merely seen him from a distance. Sholto seemed half impressed, half hostile towards him; Ambrose was something of a legend in the bank, a living myth, stalking through the marble-floored building like a modern warrior on a battlefield, with an entourage of fighting men at his heels, ready to follow him anywhere.

Sholto wanted to be like him—no, he dreamt of being him, was envious of his power, resented his authority, all at the same time.

Men had their own fantasies, myths women never shared. How could a woman understand them when she never really knew what excited, disturbed, drove them? What dreams haunted their nights and days?

She went into the *en suite* bathroom, which was far more feminine than the bedroom. The designer had gone for a warm, soothing look, cream and pink, with thick cream towels and walls the pale pink of the inside of a shell.

She looked at herself in the bathroom mirror, biting her lip. A very English reflection: the comfortable heathery tweed, the straight brown hair, the clear, creamy complexion, the blue eyes.

As if Ambrose Kerr would be remotely interested in anyone so ordinary! He had given her a lot of attention at his Christmas party, and again when he came to dinner, but it hadn't meant a thing. She should have known. Why would a man like him be interested in a girl like her?

She looked at herself scathingly. You idiot! she thought, renewing her make-up, angrily brushing her sleek brown hair. He fooled you! He was nice to you to lull Grandpa into a false sense of security. He was charming to your face, but all the time he was plotting against us.

He's treacherous. I mustn't let him take me in again!

She stared out of the bedroom window at the garden, the view of the blue hills. Winter was gentle here. The wind might be cold, but the sky was blue, the sun shone, the landscape had a soft, gracious look. There wasn't a sound to be heard. They could be a million miles from the noise and grime and bustle of London.

Why hadn't Ambrose married? Didn't he want a family, children, a real home? Did he prefer brief affairs?

Oh, stop thinking about him! she crossly told herself, but the questions didn't stop. How had he really felt about Sophie? Why had he stopped seeing her?

Suddenly she wondered . . . had he been using Sophie in some way? Using her to find out more about the Rendell family? If he had, how did Sophie feel about that? Had she been in love with him?

In Bond Street that afternoon Sophie Grant, wrapped up warmly in a long Russian-style black coat with a velvet collar, went from shop to shop looking for a pair of earrings to give her mother for Christmas; they had to look really expensive but be the opposite, because Sophie's salary at the bank was all that she and her mother had to live on, and they both liked to live well.

She paused in front of one window and gazed avidly at a wide bracelet set with diamonds and rubies; there was no price-tag but Sophie knew the lovely thing would cost more than she earned in a year.

Jewellery was a passion with her, especially rubies. They were 'her' stone; she felt drawn to them every time she saw them. She had never had any real stones; her jewellery was all costume stuff, fake, worth nothing.

She would do anything to own that bracelet. Anything. Once she had hoped that if she waited, one day...

Her full red mouth hardened. All those daydreams had been blown to dust when Emilie Madelin appeared on the scene.

Oh, she had always known George Rendell had a granddaughter over in France, but he had never mentioned her, had never visited the child. Sophie hadn't thought he intended to put her in his will. It was only when Emilie came to England and he got to know her that it dawned on Sophie that her chances of inheriting were now zilch.

The black eyes flashed bitterly. She had put in years on the old man, too. Years of dancing attendance on him, being a second daughter to him, always sweet and smiling, agreeing with everything he said.

She and her mother had really worked at it, and all for nothing. Little Miss Mouse would get it all!

'Window-shopping?' a voice behind her said, and in the window she saw Sholto Cory reflected, his blond hair ruffled by the wind, his skin flushed with cold air.

'Care to buy me that bracelet, Sholto?' she asked, lowering her lashes and looking sideways at him through them, her red mouth carefully curved in a mocking smile.

He gave it a glance, and laughed. 'You're kidding. I couldn't even afford one of those rubies! I'm not Ambrose Kerr.' He scowled. 'I couldn't even have afforded the flowers he sent Emilie the other day.'

Sophie was instantly alert. 'Did he? Why?'

'Oh, a thank-you for some dinner party her grandfather gave,' she said. Some thank-you! Ambrose sent her dozens of these perfect pink roses, God knows what they cost. Maybe if I could afford gestures like that, I'd get somewhere with her.'

'So Ambrose had dinner with George Rendell recently, did he?' Sophie's dark eyes were narrow, glittering. 'I didn't realise they socialised.'

'Nor did I,' admitted Sholto. 'But Emilie and her grandfather are visiting his place in the country this weekend, so there's something going on—maybe Ambrose has personal plans for Rendell's company?'

'The bank's arranging a take-over, surely you knew that?' Sophie said, her mind working overtime. What the devil was Ambrose up to?

She rang Gavin Wheeler the moment she got home. 'Guess who is staying with Ambrose at his place in the Cotswolds?'

'No idea, you tell me,' he said impatiently. Gavin had no love for games, except the deadly sort. He enjoyed hunting, stalking, either companies for take-over or animals with a gun; he got a thrill from a kill, thought Sophie, her red mouth smiling and her black eyes sharp. Well, so did she—they had that much in common.

'The Rendells—Emilie and the old man.'

She heard Gavin's indrawn breath. 'So,' he said, and she knew his mind too was working overtime.

'What do you think he is up to?' she asked him, thinking that she and Gavin had so much in common that they should get together more. They had worked together in the past on various projects for Ambrose. Why didn't they join forces on a project of their own?

'Maybe he plans to buy the company for himself?' Gavin thought aloud. 'But if so, why not tell me? I could help with that—why has he left me out?'

'Ask him.'

Gavin laughed angrily. 'The last time I did that he bit my head off, and he's dumped a boring, pretty low-grade job on me as some sort of punishment for arguing with him! So no, thanks, I'm not sticking my neck out again, not yet anyway. I have to ring him today or tomorrow, to give him a report, but I certainly won't be asking him any personal questions.'

'I have friends who live near Ambrose's house in the Cotswolds,' Sophie said. 'How do you feel about driving out there tomorrow? If we were visiting my friends we could drop in on Ambrose *en route*.'

'He doesn't exactly encourage visitors at that house. It is strictly his private domain. When he entertains he uses the London house. I've never actually been to the Cotswolds place.'

'You're not good enough to be invited to his home?' Sophie drawled, and heard the intake of breath which told her that her little knife had gone home.

'Obviously!' Gavin agreed in a voice that snarled. 'He wouldn't be pleased if I turned up there uninvited.'

'And you're scared of him?' Sophie mocked.

'Like hell!' Gavin muttered. 'I'm just biding my time, believe me. One day Lord High and Mighty will get a shock.'

'Well, you have to give him a report—why not in person? I'll do the talking, explain that we're visiting my friends. He won't be able to say a word, especially if we don't stay long; but we'll get some idea of what he's up to with old George and sweet little Emilie.' Her voice held acid. 'We can pool our resources, Gavin—join forces. We both have good reason to hate him.'

'What do you think is going on with the Rendells?' Gavin bluntly asked, not trusting her, not trusting anybody, come to that. The word 'trust' had not been programmed into Gavin Wheeler's computer of a brain.

'He sent her dozens of pink roses the other day.' Sophie's voice was soft and cool, but her face was as sharp as broken glass. Gavin couldn't see it, but something of her feelings must have got through to him because he gave a little whistle.

'You don't think...?' He laughed then. 'You're crazy. She's the sweet virginal type; you have to put a ring on her finger before you even get a kiss. Ambrose wouldn't look twice at her.'

'He's nearly forty—she's half his age. He has been everywhere, done everything—she's a wide-eyed innocent.' Sophie's voice grew ugly with hatred. 'It's a classic pattern.'

'You mean, he might be planning to marry her?' Gavin thought about that, whistled again. 'And you wouldn't like that!' It was his turn to stick a knife in and he enjoyed the act.

Sophie bared her teeth, but he couldn't see her, he didn't know that, and her voice gave nothing away. Sweet as honey, she cooed, 'Maybe he's planning to change his whole lifestyle. Maybe we're both going to get dumped, Gavin.'

'Maybe,' he admitted tersely, then said, 'Are you busy tonight?'

'I was planning a quiet evening at home.'

'Will you have dinner with me, instead? We have a lot to talk about.'

'Love to,' she said, smiling with satisfaction. Gavin would make a very useful ally.

When Emilie and her grandfather went back downstairs, they found Ambrose waiting in the hall by the leaping fire, one hand on the mantelshelf, staring into the flames, his hard profile lit by them, given a polished sheen.

He looked round and Emilie's heart flipped violently as their eyes met.

'Have you settled in? Rooms comfortable?' he asked.

Impulsively she said, 'My room is wonderful—I feel like the Empress Josephine!'

He said softly, 'Does that make me Napoleon?'

She swallowed, trying to sound as cool as a cucumber. 'I suppose if he was around today he would be in big business, not a soldier.'

'It's the new warfare,' he agreed, his mouth wry.

'Wasn't war always just another way of improving your trading position?' George Rendell said.

'That's the cynic's position,' Ambrose said, but he laughed. 'And you are so right. Of course it was.'

It was easier to talk than she had expected; they were all three trying not to quarrel, to keep things on a calm footing.

They ate lunch in a dining-room painted eau-de-Nil. At the windows hung pale lemon-yellow velvet curtains.

The food was beautifully cooked and delicious—balls of green melon served with poached scallops in a champagne sauce, followed by Beef Stroganoff with pilau rice, and finishing with apricot sorbet.

'Not up to your standard, I'm afraid,' Ambrose said discreetly, once Henry had served them the last course and left the room.

'It's terrific!' Emilie protested. 'Especially this sorbet...meltingly light and made with fresh fruit. You've got a very good cook.'

'Susan is good,' he agreed. 'But you are better.'

He was probably just flattering her to keep the mood friendly, but she still turned pink with pleasure. 'Do Henry and Susan stay down here, or do they go back to London when you go?'

'No, they are in charge here all year round. I have other people in London.' His tone was casual, uninterested.

George Rendell gave him a dry, sardonic look. George was comfortably off; he had a lovely home, bought a new car every year, wore good clothes, had everything he wanted—but Ambrose was seriously rich. He lived like a prince.

With all his money, why had he bothered with their company? He must be getting something out of it. George distrusted him too much now to believe that he was only doing it for the bank's investors. Had Wingate paid him a commission under the counter? Ambrose had to be making money out of the take-over.

They took their coffee in the hall by the fire. Emilie gazed into the flames while George and Ambrose talked in low, clipped tones, quietly arguing, hostility sparking between them, making her stiffen now and then, look up quickly, anxiously.

Each time Ambrose felt her movement and turned his dark head to look at her, his grey eyes brilliant in the firelight.

She met their gaze fiercely. If he upset her grandfather she would kill him, her stare said.

His mouth twisted; he said nothing, but his tone when he spoke again was more conciliatory, soothing George Rendell's ruffled feathers.

'If I agree, I shall want a contract, something put on paper,' George said flatly. 'I don't trust your word, Kerr, not any more.'

Ambrose frowned, nodded curtly, his mouth a hard line.

George stood up, rather pale now. 'I'm tired. I'd like to take a nap for an hour or so—if you don't mind?'

Emilie was immediately worried. She went upstairs with him, saw him settled on top of his bed, a quilt over him, the curtains drawn to shut out the winter afternoon.

'I shall accept his terms,' her grandfather said. 'At least I can keep an eye on what happens to our people.'

'Yes,' she said softly, kissing the top of his head.

When she returned downstairs Ambrose suggested they take a walk. They put on coats, gloves, scarves, and explored the gardens, which were even more extensive than she had realised, surrounding the whole house on all sides, with a high stone wall forming the outer limit.

'You said something about painting,' she reminded him, and he shrugged, glancing at the pale blue of the sky.

'The light will be fading within an hour—it will be the shortest day in the year soon, remember—and to catch the light at its best you have to start early in the morning. I thought we could have breakfast at eight tomorrow and start work immediately afterwards. We could work on a still life—some fruit, a bowl, a couple of jugs, nothing difficult.'

'I'm not very good at proportions,' she confessed.

'Doesn't matter. You'll soon learn how to work them out,' he promised as they followed winding paths which ran between herbaceous borders and banks of rhododendron, past a sunken garden which was laid out with rose-beds, and through a wild garden, planted with some young hazel trees and currant bushes. A few snowdrops, pure white buds and green tips, showed among the skeletal leaves of autumn which were still dying back into the earth.

'Nothing much to see at this time of year,' he told her. 'You must come in spring, when the daffodils and hyacinths are out—or in bluebell time. Under the trees the bluebells are as thick as grass for weeks, a sea of deep blue, quite magical. After that we have the magnolias, the camellias, the azaleas... and later still the roses, of course.'

They sat down under the wooden arches of the sunken rose-garden, where climbing roses had been trained to grow up a pergola. There was one lonely white rose on a bush nearby.

'Oh, look,' she said. 'How lovely! The last rose—it looks lonely.'

Ambrose leaned over, broke off the stem, and handed her the flower.

'Oh, you shouldn't have... Your last rose...' she protested, startled.

She was so taken aback that she buried her face in it. There was no perfume, but the feel of the white petals on her lips was strangely evocative.

'Does it have a scent?' asked Ambrose, and she shook her head, holding out the rose.

He took it back from her, his fingers cool against her warmer skin, sending a shiver down her spine.

She watched him lift the rose to his nostrils. 'No, no scent at all,' he agreed, and then, deliberately, let the petals drift across his own mouth, as they had over hers.

She felt her insides go hollow; weakness made her tremble, made her eyes darken so that she saw him through a smoky mist.

It frightened her; she began to talk to cover her deep awareness of him, babbling, her voice shaky.

'Did you live in the country when you were a child?'

He dropped the rose into her lap. 'No.'

The terse monosyllable made her stiffen; she picked up the rose and a thorn ran into her finger.

She gave a little cry, dropping the rose again.

'Did you prick yourself?'

Ambrose slid along the bench, took her hand in his and lifted the finger so that he could see it.

'You're bleeding!'

He bent his dark head; she drew a shaken breath as he softly licked the blood away. There was a brief pause, then he very slowly sucked her finger right into his mouth.

Emilie was trembling. It was only what you might do to a child who had pricked its finger, and yet... and yet there was something very different here. It was intense, intimate, almost shocking, the feel of that warm moistness surrounding her finger, sucking softly at her.

His mouth parted again and released her finger. 'Better?' he murmured.

She couldn't get a word out.

He lifted his head; his face was pale, his eyes dark, all pupil, glistening like jet. He was breathing thickly.

Emilie went into panic; she jumped up and began to run, but Ambrose caught up with her, grabbed her arm to halt her, staring at her averted face.

'Don't look like that!' he muttered.

'Let go of me, then!' She was trembling.

'What do you think I'm going to do to you?' His voice was harsh with anger.

She shot a nervous glance through her lashes at him. His face was brooding, the set of his mouth savage. He frightened her.

He suddenly burst out, 'You're so damned young. Why...? God, I keep forgetting...'

She pulled herself free, blundered away like a moth from a flame, drawn to him irresistibly and yet afraid of what might happen to her if she got too close.

He moved too, at the same instant, and they collided, their bodies touching, and Emilie looked up, lips parted, gasping, dazed, as helpless to save herself as someone drowning.

Ambrose made a deep, thick sound, his skin darkly flushed, his eyes fixed on her mouth.

Her mind clouded. She stopped trying to think. Hypnotised, she watched his mouth descend as it took hers. At the first touch of it her eyes closed; darkness dropped over her, a darkness split in the same instant by a blinding flash of light. I'm in love, she thought, appalled.

She couldn't be. Not with this man, of all men. He was the last man in the world she should fall in love with. He was their enemy; she couldn't trust him. All he would do was hurt her. She must be crazy.

She opened her eyes. The world was spinning; she had vertigo. She dazedly pushed him away, broke out wildly, 'I don't want you touching me!'

Ambrose looked almost as dazed as she felt, his face darkly flushed. He stared down at her as if he didn't understand what she had said.

She began to run back to the house, wanting to cry and wishing she were alone, so that she could give way to the misery engulfing her. Why had she fallen in love with the man responsible for taking her family firm away? If Grandpa so much as guessed, he would see her as a traitor too. He would never forgive her.

She heard Ambrose coming behind her, his long strides almost silent as he ran across grass to catch up with her. Emilie felt the panic of something small and helpless being hunted by a ruthless predator.

A scream rose in her throat; she choked it back. She leapt up some steps and slipped on wet leaves. She just saved herself by catching hold of a bush, but fell into it, entangled in bare branches.

Ambrose caught up.

'Are you hurt?' he asked urgently, putting his fingers under her chin and raising her face so that he could look at it.

'No,' she whispered, her lashes down because she couldn't meet his gaze. Her whole body was deeply aware of him; she hadn't recovered yet from that kiss, the consuming heat of his mouth.

'I'm sorry if I scared you,' he said in a low, deep voice.

She felt him watching her, and her heart beat heavily. She pulled free and began to walk back towards the house; he fell into step beside her. Neither of them said anything.

She couldn't bear the tension; she had to say something, anything. But her mind had gone blank; how could she think clearly when all her concentration was dominated by what was happening to her body?

'Why did you choose banking as a career?' The minute the words were out, she could have kicked herself. It was such a dumb question.

'I didn't,' he said at once, though, as if her question had been a relief, and perhaps he was as troubled by the strange, barbed silence between them as she had been. 'It just happened by accident. I trained as an accountant, for a while, and studied law. I got into banking through meeting an amazing old man called Harry Weiner, who talked me into taking a job in his merchant bank. I've been lucky in meeting the right people at the right time.' He paused, frowning into the distance. 'Life balances out in the strangest way.'

'Does it?' What was he talking about? she wondered, watching him with fascination. His face, his body, had such power, a strength which she sensed went deeper than she could see. He was an iceberg, glittering and deadly, with only a fraction of himself showing above the surface.

'When I was young I had no idea what was ahead for me,' he said, almost to himself, staring at his house, at the beautiful, elegant gardens around it. 'If anyone had told me I wouldn't have believed them. This place, for instance—now and then I wonder if I'm imagining that I live here, if this place really belongs to me. If I had had second sight it would have made my childhood a damn sight easier to bear.'

Tentatively, she asked him, 'Were you poor when you were young?'

He laughed harshly. 'Poor? The word doesn't cover it. The past is a nightmare I have now and then ... when I'm upset, when I'm worried ... I go back in my sleep and the shock is terrible. My life was hell for so long. I was working by the time I was ten years old, working from sun-up to midnight and sleeping in a one-room shack shared by eight others...'

Emilie's eyes had widened until they hurt; she must have made an incredulous sound, although she wasn't aware of it, because Ambrose suddenly stopped and looked at her, turning white.

'I've never told a living soul any of that before,' he muttered, and the whiteness of his face was slowly invaded by dark red.

She stared up at him, blue eyes echoing the shock in his own as what he had told her reverberated in her mind. She hadn't yet really taken it all in—where on earth could he have come from to have lived like that, to have been working at such an early age?

He ran a hand through his thick black hair in an angry gesture. 'God knows why I blurted it out to you. I wonder if you realise... I've given you a weapon that could destroy me. These men I work with every day have all grown up with silver spoons in their mouths, they went to the same schools, talk with the same plummy voices, their families know each other, they're a tribal clan, they only like each other, trust each other. If they suspected where I came from, what my life has been like, they would know I was an outsider in their cosy world, not one of their old-boy network; they'd turn on me, rip me to pieces. So if you want to ruin me, you only have to repeat to one of them what I just told you.'

CHAPTER FIVE

THEY spent the next morning painting, in the large conservatory at one side of the house. There were still a few flowers in there—some house-plants, bowls of hyacinths and daffodils, ferns, a small orange-tree in a tub, and a trained vine, which in summer, Ambrose said, grew up the walls and across the glass roof, but which now was leafless and had been cut right back.

The centre of the conservatory was empty, leaving plenty of room for Ambrose to set up their easels. The morning light was clear and bright, although outside it was freezing, a white frost stiffening the grass into spikes which crunched underfoot.

They both painted a still-life Ambrose had set up on a table in front of them: oranges and lemons in a smooth, blue-glazed bowl, a book lying next to them.

Ambrose came over to see how she was doing, and put his arms round her to make a few quick, deft changes to her picture. 'Something like that might be better?'

She nodded. 'I see what you mean, thank you,' she said huskily, intensely aware of the warmth of his body close to her, the strength of it there for her to lean on. She longed to turn into him, cling, bury herself in him. He moved away and she felt cold. She made herself concentrate on what she was trying to do. Her second attempt was much better. She could see his canvas out of the corner of her eye; the vivid fruit was there already, hot glowing orange, clear cool lemon. The painting was bold, passionate, startling.

He was a very surprising man. Everything she found out about him was a surprise. Look at what he had told her yesterday! She still hadn't recovered from the shock of hearing about his childhood.

He had looked into her eyes, his face dark, tense, the bones seeming almost to thrust through his tight skin, and she had stared back in stunned silence.

Around them the twilight had been thickening, blue and smoky, in a moment of enchantment, and then from the house her grandfather had called and the moment had been shattered.

Ambrose leaned over to look at her picture again. 'Come on, give us lots of colour, this isn't a water-colour!'

She laughed, slapping yellow on to the canvas with her knife, and he nodded.

'Better! Think where the fruit comes from—hot countries, full of colour and life. That's what you want to convey.'

'Is that where you were born? A hot country?' The question was out before she could stop it and she gasped afterwards, stricken. 'I'm sorry...I shouldn't have asked... Don't be angry!'

He had stiffened, she had felt his body turn rigid behind her, and the shock of it had gone through her too. She had begun to tremble.

His hands fell on her shoulders and she started vi-olently, turning white.

He swung her round and she dropped her palette-knife on to the floor, her frightened eyes lifting to take in the tension of his face.

'Don't!'

His eyes flashed over her pallor, her wide darkened eyes, her trembling mouth.

'For God's sake!' he muttered. 'What's wrong now?' Every conversation they ever had seemed to break down into one of these moments of tension.

'You looked so angry,' she half explained, half accused, then sighed. 'It was my fault—I shouldn't have asked you about your childhood. I know it upsets you to talk about it.'

He looked away from her, his black brows level above his grey eyes, his cheekbones taut, his mouth a hard line. She watched him with anxiety. What was he thinking about? Was he remembering? Remembering the past he had said was a nightmare?

'I never have talked about it,' he said, then looked back at her, his eyes searching her face. 'Maybe if I had it wouldn't haunt my dreams.'

'Maybe you should?' she tentatively began, then stopped, afraid to go on in case he bit her head off.

He looked sombre, his mouth twisting. 'Maybe I should,' he agreed, then let go of her and walked back to his own easel. 'Shall we get on with our painting?'

Dazedly, she looked about for her palette-knife, remembered she had dropped it, hunted on the floor and found it, wiped it clean and began to load it with paint again, all her movements automatic, unthinking.

She worked on the blue of the bowl for some minutes, puzzling over the problem of getting the shine of light on the curve of it.

Ambrose's voice made her start.

'You're right about my being born in a hot country— I was born in Mexico,' he said, and her head lifted, her hair flicking back from her face as she turned to look at him, startled by the sudden admission. What had made him decide to tell her that?

He wasn't looking at her; he was staring at the canvas in front of him, using the edge of his knife to block in the edge of a shape, his dark head tilted as he looked from his picture to the still-life on the table.

He talked flatly, quietly. 'My father was an Englishman called Andrew Kerr. He went out to Mexico a couple of years before I was born, prospecting for oil. He met my mother there. She was Mexican—she worked in the hotel where he was living. She got pregnant, he married her and I arrived. A few months later he lost his job with the company who had taken him out there. He managed to get other jobs, but he had started to drink. He only kept jobs for a few months, sometimes just weeks. Sooner or later he would go off on a drinking jag and he'd be fired. We lived hand to mouth. It wasn't easy for my mother, especially as—when he was drunk— my father was violent.'

She didn't make a sound, but he must have picked up what she was feeling because he turned his head to look at her.

Her blue eyes were dark, compassionate. She was thinking about the little boy he must have been—what a terrible childhood! No wonder he didn't like talking about it.

'He hit her?' she whispered.

'He hit all of us,' Ambrose said in a voice made rough by pain and anger, then broke off, his teeth tight and his face drawn and tense.

She impulsively went to him, put a comforting hand on his shoulder. 'I'm sorry.'

He gave her hand a sideways glance through his lashes. Emilie felt heat flare between them as instantly as if she had lit a match and set fire to them both.

Drawing a sharp breath, she hurriedly stopped touching him.

Ambrose's eyes had darkened. Roughly he said, 'I don't know why I'm telling you all this . . . I didn't mean to. I never talk about it, I never have before, to anyone.'

Very flushed, she broke out, 'Don't tell me if it upsets you, but . . . if you want to talk, I'd like to hear about it.'

His eyes searched her face again. Emilie must still be angry because the bank had arranged a take-over of her family firm, yet he couldn't see hostility in her face any more. Was she pretending to be interested in him? But she looked so innocent, with her wide blue eyes and gentle smile.

Can I trust her? he thought grimly. Ambrose trusted very few people; the dark world he had come from had taught him to rely on himself, never on anyone else. Especially women. Most of those he met lied and cheated to get what they wanted. Her cousin, Sophie, for instance . . . he wouldn't trust her for an instant.

His face tightened. I should never have told Emilie that if she wanted to destroy me she only had to tell everyone where I come from! I put a weapon in her hands.

But would she use it?

She was looking up at him uncertainly, aware of the hard grey eyes, the ruthless features. Ambrose had the look of someone fighting continually to keep all his emotions battened down, hidden away. Was that part of the legacy of his terrible childhood? Was he afraid to remember? She winced, torn with compassion for him.

'I'm sorry I asked you . . .' she whispered, moving closer again, her blue eyes shimmering with pity.

Ambrose's body was torn by desire so sharp that he couldn't speak until he had fought it down. He raked back his thick black hair, his hand not quite steady.

His nostrils inhaled the scent of her: she smelt of spring. He wanted her so much it was agony; he ached to bury himself in her. Heat burned low inside him. If only she weren't so young. But was she *too* young?

Swallowing, he averted his eyes and muttered, 'It isn't a romantic story, Emilie, if that's what you think. I'm not the hero of a fairy-story. My life has been an endless struggle right back from the beginning. I'm tough because I've had to be. We're like pearls; we start off as a tiny grain of sand and every second of our lives adds another layer to us without our realising what is happening. I hated my father for years, and I still do, I suppose, but I understand him better now. He was violent because he was a disappointed and angry man. He had ruined his own life, but that didn't make it any easier for him to bear. The worse things got the more he drank, the more he drank the more violent he became.'

She sucked in her breath and he looked at her, mouth twisting cynically.

'I told you this wasn't a pretty story. Once he beat my mother up so badly that she lost the baby she was carrying. She said she had tripped, but we all knew the truth. That was when I really started to hate my father. She almost died. My mother had a baby every year or so— it began to break her health. She was a tiny little woman, fragile and gentle. She sang when she was happy, which wasn't often, but even when she was tired or ill she was full of love. She never complained. She prayed, lit candles in church, offered up all her problems to the Virgin Mary. It didn't seem to help. The problems didn't go away.'

There was bitter cynicism in his voice, and under that Emilie heard the pain again.

'Maybe it helped her bear them, though?' she gently suggested, and he gave her a quick frowning look, his mouth twisting.

'Maybe it did.' There was a faint surprise in his voice as if that had never occurred to him.

'You loved her very much, didn't you?' Emilie was touched by the idea of his love for his mother. She wished she had known her.

His face was grim. 'Yes. It nearly drove me mad not to be able to do anything to make her life easier. I was too young to stop him hitting her; when I tried he beat me up and it made it worse for her. She begged me not to interfere again—she was afraid he might kill me.' His mouth twisted. 'I dreamt of killing him, when I was big enough, but I never had to. He was killed in a mining accident when I was ten. We had travelled all over Mexico by then, living in rented places. I hadn't had much education—there was barely time for me to start school somewhere before we moved on again—but while my father was alive we managed to stay just above starvation level. When he died we had nothing, not a penny. There were seven of us, and the landlord told us to get out of the place we had been renting.'

'Wasn't there anyone who would help you? What about your mother's family?'

'We'd long ago lost contact with them. They hadn't wanted her to marry my father, she wasn't married in a church because my father was not a religious man, so her family didn't want anything to do with her after that. She wouldn't go to them for help.'

'Your father's family?'

'We never knew where they lived; he never told us. When he died, I had to take over as head of the family. I was the eldest—I had to start earning enough for all of us. I'd already been earning a little, since I was eight or so, picking over garbage from the dumps——'

She caught her breath and he looked at her, his mouth grim.

'Yes,' he said tersely. 'It was a disgusting job; I worked waist-deep in filth for hours. In summer the smell turned your stomach and you were covered in flies.'

She had turned pale. 'How terrible... Children—such young children... But didn't anyone know it was happening? Didn't anyone try to stop it?'

He laughed shortly, his face grim. 'Everyone knew, of course they did, but it made money, and the really poor in countries like Mexico have a choice of starving to death or doing filthy jobs to earn enough to eat.'

'But didn't the police...?'

'The police?' His smile made her wince. 'They turned a blind eye, or took a cut—they certainly didn't interfere.'

She swallowed. 'It must have been... How could you bear it?'

He shrugged. 'You got used to it—to the smell of the place, the rats...'

'Rats?' She shuddered.

He nodded. 'The whole place was alive with them—and with flies. They laid their eggs in the rotting food—in summer the dump writhed with maggots.'

She retched, was almost sick, her hand going to her mouth, her face white and sweating.

Ambrose swore under his breath, put an arm round her and held her up as she swayed.

'I knew I shouldn't have told you!' he broke out harshly. 'That's enough. I'm not talking about it any more. Do you want to lie down?'

'No, I'll be OK in a minute,' she whispered, leaning on him, turning her face towards the warmth of him. His throat was firm and strong; she inhaled the scent of his skin. If she moved an inch she would have her mouth against it. Yearning rose up inside her in a tidal wave.

He was breathing rapidly, irregularly, as if he knew what she was feeling. His hand moved up and down her spine comfortingly as he murmured into the top of her head, his mouth against her soft brown hair.

'I'm sorry, I wish to God I'd never started telling you!'

'I wanted to know... I'm glad you told me...'

She shut her eyes, her whole body lying heavily against him. Her mouth touched his throat.

He drew a sharp breath. The hand stroking her began to move in a different way. The gentle comfort became sensual, the fingers splayed, touched with a feeling that made every nerve-end in her body prickle with intense sensation.

'It must have been a nightmare,' she said, her lips moving so close to his neck that her breathing was warm on his skin.

His voice was hushed, husky. 'It was—it still is, in a way. I often have nightmares about being back there. But I shouldn't have told you. I didn't want any of it to touch you. It was bad enough having to live through it myself; I didn't want you even to know about it. I still don't know why I started telling you—it was the last thing I meant to do.'

'You needed to talk about it. Everyone needs to talk; it isn't good to lock things up inside you,' she said gently. 'I'm glad you picked me. I only wish I hadn't spoilt it by being stupid.' She lifted her head reluctantly, wishing she dared openly kiss his neck, wanting to stay there all day, her mouth buried against his skin.

Ambrose looked down at her, his eyes dark, glittering, like black stars. 'You're so sensitive, and very young, and you've led a sheltered life—you've never had to face anything like that.'

'I nursed my mother until she died,' she quietly said. 'It was a long, slow, painful death, and I was on my own for most of the time.'

'I'd forgotten,' he said, wincing. 'It doesn't show in your face.'

She smiled wryly. 'Doesn't it? But it's there, under the skin, all those months of worry and fear and being so sad without being able to cry in case she saw me.'

'What about your father? Where was he?'

'Either at work, or with the woman he married almost as soon as my mother was buried.' Her tone was flat, almost expressionless.

He was silent.

She smiled at him. 'You see, we have something in common—neither of us liked our fathers much.'

He brushed the soft brown hair back from her face, his fingers lingering on her cheek as he smiled at her. Her heart was jumping around inside her like a frog; she hoped he couldn't hear it.

There was a sound behind them. Ambrose moved away swiftly, stiffening. Very pink, Emilie looked round towards the door into the house.

Henry stood there, and behind him were other faces. For a second Emilie was so disturbed that she didn't recognise them.

'Miss Grant, Mr Wheeler, and Mr Cory, sir,' Henry said in a blank, level voice, but his eyes were intent, curious.

Ambrose's brows met, heavy and menacing above ice-floes of grey eyes. Emilie had never seen him look like that and it was a shock.

'This is a surprise,' he said, and his voice sent a shiver down Emilie's spine; she was glad she was not on the receiving end of that tone.

She met Sophie's black eyes and got another shock, a deeper one, which sent alarm reverberating through her, made her turn white. Sophie was looking at her as if she hated her.

She's jealous! thought Emilie, startled. Of me!

'We are on our way to lunch with friends,' Gavin Wheeler said in a cheerful, bluff voice which didn't ring true. 'I have those papers with me—I was going to fax them to you, but they are very confidential.' He pulled a briefcase from under his arm, unzipped it and got out a black file of papers. He held it towards Ambrose, smiling broadly, without real warmth, a smile that was all teeth and no depth. 'Realising how close we were going to be to your house, I decided to drop them in on you myself.'

Ambrose took the file, then dropped it on the dark green table at which they had drunk their coffee.

'You should have faxed them,' he said through his teeth.

Sholto was staring fixedly at Emilie, who met his eyes for a second then looked away in a hurry. Sholto was furious because he had seen her in Ambrose's arms; his face was sharp with jealousy. Emilie didn't want to encourage Sholto, but she hated to see pain in his eyes. She didn't want to cause pain to anyone.

Sophie sauntered into the conservatory, saw the two easels set up and walked over to them, staring, lifting perfectly shaped brows, laughing lightly, with mockery beneath the laughter.

'Ambrose! I didn't know you painted! You're full of surprises.'

The barbed tone made his frown deepen. 'So are you, Sophie,' he drawled. 'I had no idea you and Gavin were ... friends.'

Sophie's eyes flashed briefly, then her lashes lowered over them, and she laughed lightly again.

'And I had no idea you and my little cousin knew each other so well, either.'

'There's a lot about me you don't know,' Ambrose said angrily.

Sophie's eyes held a curious gleam. 'I can't wait to find out.'

Ambrose tensed. 'Be careful, Sophie. Remember what happened to the cat.'

She lifted one brow. 'The cat?'

'Curiosity killed it.'

'Oh, don't worry, I'll be careful!' Sophie said sweetly.

The other man held out a hand to Emilie, giving her his false, cold smile, from which she flinched as from the smile of a shark. 'We haven't been introduced ... I'm Gavin Wheeler. I work for Ambrose.'

She murmured her own name. His skin was clammy; she withdrew her hand as soon as she politely could.

Sophie was inspecting Emilie's canvas now, her brows arched. 'Is Ambrose giving you lessons?' She slid a sideways look at him. 'Are you giving her private lessons, Ambrose?'

There were undertones in everything she said; Emilie heard them and blushed.

Ambrose was grim, his eyes smouldering, his body tense with rage barely under control.

Sophie seemed unworried by that glare. She smilingly wandered off to look at the flowers in the conservatory, bending to breathe in their scent.

'I'd like a quick word about those papers, before we go,' Gavin said, and the two men moved off to the far end of the conservatory and talked in low voices.

'Was he kissing you? What's going on, Em?' muttered Sholto, his face reproachful.

'Don't make a scene, Sholto!' she hissed, and began painting again, turning her back on him.

He grabbed her arm to swing her round to face him. 'You're my girl, we've been dating for ages—I've a right to know what's going on!'

She tried to pull away, flushing with anger. 'I am not yours, Sholto!'

He descended to pleading, looking at her miserably. 'Don't dump me for him, Em. I love you.'

She sighed at the look on his face, sorry for him again. 'Sholto, I'm sorry, I don't want to hurt you, but...'

'Oh, Em,' he groaned, and tried to kiss her. She pushed him away, and in the struggle her easel was almost knocked over.

Ambrose swung round, glaring, then strode back towards them.

'What the hell do you think you're doing, Cory?' he grated, his face darkly flushed with anger.

Sholto let go of her, but bristled with resentment at Ambrose's tone. 'She's my girl, I can kiss her if I like!'

Ambrose shot her a look, his eyes hot with fury. 'Did you want him to kiss you?'

Sophie intervened before she could answer. 'Darling, girls of Emilie's age never know what they want! They're always changing their minds and playing hard to get!'

He slowly detached his intense stare from Emilie's face, and frowned at the other woman. 'Didn't you say you were on your way to lunch with someone? It's half-past twelve. Shouldn't you be going?'

'Oh, this is a very casual lunch—the Randoms, at Abbot's Mead. Have you been there at the weekend? They never get up before noon and then they eat around the pool—a buffet meal, everyone helps themselves after a swim.'

'At this time of year?' Ambrose raised his black eyebrows and looked out at the frozen weather, incredulous.

'The Randoms have a heated pool-house—it's like being in the south of France in August, darling! You'd love it.' Sophie's voice dripped honey, but it was poisoned honey. 'Anyway, we have plenty of time for a drink with you before we have to go!'

His profile was razor-sharp. Emilie thought for a moment that he was going to refuse, but instead he said, 'Come into the drawing-room.' He gave Emilie a quick look. 'You've got paint on your face and hands—why not run upstairs and wash your hands, get rid of all the paint, before lunch?'

Emilie was glad to escape. She politely smiled at the other two. 'Nice to meet you, Mr Wheeler. Have a good lunch, Sophie.'

'See you soon, darling,' Sophie breathed, flipping dark red nails at her. 'We must have lunch and talk girl-talk.'

Emilie forced another smile, then threw a brief look at Sholto. 'And you, Sholto.'

He began to follow her. She stopped, looking up at him, her face wistful, pleading. 'Please don't say anything else, Sholto. We've said everything there is to say.'

Ambrose watched them both with hard, narrowed eyes, and Sophie watched him. Was that jealousy she saw in his face? If she weren't so furious, she would laugh at the thought of Ambrose feeling jealousy. He's human after all, she thought, her teeth tight. Well, well, well. Imagine that. He has blood. I hope I'm going to see him bleed.

She had dreamt of marrying him once, of living in that beautiful Regency house in Regent's Park, having everything she had ever wanted... all the jewellery and furs and beautiful things she had dreamt of all her life. She had even begun to take on the persona of the future Mrs Kerr at the bank; she had enjoyed seeing the reactions of her colleagues when it dawned on them that one day she might be their boss's wife.

Ambrose had made her fall from a great height when he dropped her. He had humiliated her in front of everyone. She had never let her chagrin show. She had smiled and smiled, and hidden away her real feelings. But from then on she had hated him and dreamt of seeing him suffer.

Ambrose was completely unaware of Sophie's watchful gaze, let alone her tortuous emotions. He couldn't hear what Sholto and Emilie were saying, but he saw Sholto touch her hand and she didn't snatch it away—she let him hold those slender, delicate fingers, let him lift them to his mouth.

He felt his stomach clench.

'Aren't they sweet together?' cooed Sophie, smiling. 'Young love. Doesn't it make you wish you were that young again?'

Ambrose turned a glance on her that even Sophie found alarming. Her smile withered, she took a step back, sucking in breath like someone suddenly confronted by a wild beast.

Sholto whispered, 'I'm sorry for upsetting you—please stop punishing me. I love you, Em. I really love you, it's churning my guts to think of you with him.'

'Don't be silly, Sholto! Nothing's going on between us... You're crazy! Me and Ambrose!' She pretended to laugh, but there was a strange fever running through her veins and she didn't stop him when he took her hand. What had Sholto noticed in Ambrose's face, in his voice when he spoke to her? Or had Sholto just picked up on her feelings? 'What on earth makes you think he...might like me?' she asked him breathlessly.

'I've got eyes,' he said sulkily, looking like a little boy again. 'Em, he's too old for you! Why are you staying here? What's going on?'

'Nothing, this is just business,' she said, and Sholto cheered up a little.

'Is this to do with the Wingate take-over? I heard about that. Is your grandfather making a deal with Kerr? That's good.' He lifted her hand and kissed it quickly before she could pull it away. 'Oh, well, if that's all! Sorry I was stupid. Can I see you next week, then? Dinner? A play?'

'Ring me. I don't know when I'm free—I'll have to look at my diary,' she said evasively, and fled.

In her room she had a quick shower and changed into a powder-blue silk tunic dress, brushed her hair, put on make-up. She looked into the mirror, and her reflection made her heart sink. She was just a very thin, very young girl, without glamour or sophistication. Why on earth should a man like Ambrose be interested in her, when there was someone like Sophie around?

Sophie's stunning, magnetic, sexy. And she's still in love with him! That's why she looked at me as if she hated me just now. She's jealous. As if she needs to be! I'm no competition for her.

Depression settled on her like grey ash. She heard a car driving away—they had gone, then? She would have to go downstairs, join the two men, but she didn't want to.

She found George Rendell sitting in front of the hall fire, sipping a glass of whisky. He looked round and gave her his loving smile.

'There you are, darling! Do you want a drink? Sherry? A glass of wine?' He knew she would not drink spirits.

She shook her head. 'No, thanks, Grandpa.' She sat down opposite him.

He said wryly, 'Surprised to see Sophie turning up with young Cory and that chap Wheeler. Never liked him much—not quite sure what he does for Ambrose. Researcher, Ambrose calls him, but what does that mean? Don't trust the man. Got shifty eyes. Do you think Sophie is dating him? Of course, she's a girl with an eye to the main chance, and Wheeler is one of those powers behind the throne, sort of chap who can become pretty important. Find a lot of them in politics—dirty business, politics. Suits men like Wheeler.'

Emilie held out her cold hands to the log fire, watching the blue flames as if she could see something in them.

'Sophie dated Ambrose, didn't she?' She couldn't stop herself imagining it—Sophie and Ambrose in bed together. They had been to bed, she just knew it, and it made her sick with jealousy.

'Oh, she had her eye on him—for all I know she still has—but Sophie's a realist. If she is sure she can't have Ambrose she'll look around for someone else.'

They both heard Ambrose on the stairs, which killed the subject. Although he was perfectly polite and friendly to them both, there was something hard in his eyes that made Emilie shiver whenever she met his glance. His mood now was quite different from the way he had been before Sophie's arrival. How did he really feel about Sophie? Was he still half in love with her? But why had they stopped seeing each other, in that case?

She wished she knew Ambrose better, but there was always a sense of something hidden about him, as if his face were a hard, blank wall between everyone he met and the secret part of him.

After lunch, George Rendell went off upstairs to lie down for an hour, and Ambrose and Emilie returned to the conservatory.

The light was no longer so good, but they had little left to do. Emilie waited a while before hesitantly saying, 'Would you finish your story? You didn't tell me what happened after your father died?'

He frowned heavily at the canvas, not looking at her. 'I don't want to bore you.'

'You won't bore me,' she said quietly.

He shot her a look, then was silent for a while before slowly picking up his story. 'I needed to earn enough to keep the family once my father was gone. I had to find rent, for the even cheaper place we managed to find, and money for food. We got our clothes from the dump, of course.' He gave her a bitter little smile. 'None of us ever had new clothes; everything we wore came from the dump. It's amazing what people throw away in a big city; sometimes I found stuff that looked quite good when it was washed. I had to fight for what I found, of course. I couldn't just keep it. We had a strict system about that. It was supposed to come out of our share of the money we were paid by the dealers. But I was bigger and tougher—I scared the other boys into letting me keep what I wanted. Then I moved on from picking over the dump to sorting out what the other boys found. It was simple enough—you put bottles in one pile, old clothes in another, newspapers here, broken furniture there—almost all of it was worth something to someone. It was all recycled. The guy who employed me sold it on, of course. I got very good at sorting the stuff—the faster you worked, the more you earned. I was soon his best worker. After a couple of years I realised how the system worked, and I began to see how I could earn even more.'

'How old were you?'

'Twelve by then.' He shrugged.

She looked at him with silent awe. How could a child that young have been so shrewd and determined?

He was unaware of her eyes. Frowning, as if looking back down a long, dark tunnel, he was too absorbed in his own memories. 'I found out who bought the stuff from the man who paid me, and I started out on my own account. I bought from the boys on the dump, at a slightly higher price than he paid. I had boys sorting it for me, and I sold at a lower price than my old boss was asking.'

'How did he take it?'

Ambrose laughed harshly. 'He tried to kill me.'

She caught her breath. 'To kill you?' He had said it so offhandedly, as if it happened every day.

'He and his brother came looking for me—but I'd been expecting them. I had an early-warning system set up—my brothers kept watch on them and ran like hell to let me know they were on their way. I knew a policeman who lived nearby. I called him and he got there a few minutes after they did. They had begun beating me up by then—oh, I could have hidden, but then the police would have had nothing to hold them on, so I stayed around and let them attack me. I had a little gang of other boys to help me, hold them off until the policeman got there. On my own, I couldn't have fought them, but we chucked things at them—we'd stockpiled some rocks, rotten food, a few broken bricks. I spent a week in hospital, I still have a knife-scar on my chest, but I survived. My brothers ran the business for me until I came out. The two men went to prison for attempted murder.'

'And the authorities still did nothing to stop you working on the dumps?' She was shocked, incredulous.

He gave her a sardonic, almost pitying look. 'Mexico was—still is—a very poor country with a lot of problems. The state didn't have the resources to deal with us. There are plenty of places in South America today where you would see kids aged ten, and a lot less, doing the same job I did. You haven't been over there, you have no idea what it's like—the poverty, the overcrowding, the home-lessness, the cardboard shacks millions live in, around the edges of huge cities—most kids never break out of it, even if they live to grow up, and many don't.'

She winced. 'It sounds terrible. I know the mortality-rate in third-world countries is very high among children.'

'Not high enough for some people,' he bit out, face grim. 'In some South American countries men go out at night with guns, hunting down street kids—seven-year-olds, nine-year-olds. They've lived on the streets all their lives and these are pretty dangerous kids—they come out of dark alleys and knife people for a pathetic sum of money. They're not like children at all; they've led such terrible lives they're like rats, killer rats. Nobody knows how to deal with them, so they kill them. That's one method of dealing with street crime. It's quick and it's cheap.'

Emilie looked at him, eyes dark. 'That's horrific! Surely somebody could do something?'

'I've started a foundation which I hope will do something, once it is up and running. But even that is getting bogged down in bureaucracy; the people who will be in charge never stop arguing about the best way of dealing with the problem—building new orphanages, giving money to established ones, offering birth-control advice. They have plenty of ideas, they just can't agree on which to go for. And meanwhile the problem is getting worse every day.'

'At least you're doing something. Can't you insist on the way the money is spent?'

'It isn't that easy. I only wish it was.'

There was a little silence. 'What about your mother, your brothers and sisters?' she asked. 'Where are they now?'

His face altered. 'My mother's dead. She and my two brothers died when the shack we were living in caught fire.'

Emilie looked at him in horror. 'Oh, how terrible!'

'It happened all the time; the shacks were flimsy, cardboard affairs. A cooking-stove overturned, they said. I was at work. I came back to find myself homeless, and my three sisters gone. They had been taken away by the police, put in a convent orphanage for girls. I was thirteen by then—I thought of myself as a man. I had been taking care of the family for three years, and I was earning quite well, but I was still a minor so the police took me off to an orphanage for boys. I ran away that night. I found the orphanage where they had my sisters, and managed to get to see them secretly. I wanted them to come away with me, but they preferred to stay where they were.'

She heard the hardness in his voice and winced for him. 'And it hurt you?'

'It meant that I was alone,' he said flatly. 'From then on I only had myself to worry about; life was easier.'

She wasn't deceived by his offhand manner. 'So what happened to them?'

'I didn't see them for years.'

Emilie watched him, seeing the pain in his eyes and aching for him. 'You were too hurt?'

He gave her a twisted smile, his eyes sardonic. 'I felt they'd rejected me,' he admitted. 'Yes, I was hurt, and angry, and bitter. But I got over it, in time; I went back, years later, to look for them.'

'Did you find them?'

He nodded. 'Two of them had married—Maria and Juanita. They had grown fat, and had half a dozen children. They still live in Mexico. I keep in touch with them. My elder sister, Consuela, became a nun—she liked the life, God knows why.'

'Maybe she liked the stability and security it gave her after all those years of moving from place to place, never quite knowing what might happen next,' Emilie softly suggested, and he laughed, nodding.

'She certainly got fed well in there—she had been a tiny, skinny shrimp of a girl, but they soon had her looking plump and rosy, and they were kind, those women. That's why my sisters wouldn't leave with me.

Like stray cats, they had found a good home, and wanted to stay in it.'

'Can you blame them?'

He looked sombre. 'No. But they were my family and they had rejected me. It wounded my pride. I was the man of the family, I wanted to take care of them, but they didn't trust me to do it. But now I'm really a man I can see I wasn't thinking of them at all, only of myself.'

There was that haunted look in his eyes; she was beginning to recognise it. At first she had thought he was impervious, a man used to authority, with no weaknesses. She should have remembered that he was a human being, not some flawless machine. He had had a harsh, difficult life. No wonder he was bitter.

'When did you first come to England?'

'When I was sixteen. I realised I had dual nationality, so I applied for a copy of my birth certificate and then got a British passport. It took some time—bureaucracy again. I had to prove my identity. Once I had my passport, I got a job on a cruise-ship. On board, I met a kind-hearted couple from Liverpool. He was an accountant, she was a nurse; they had no children. It was a month's cruise; I got to know them pretty well and he offered me a job if I ever came to England.'

'What sort of job?'

'Office work, he said. I took him at his word. We kept in touch by letter, and the first time we docked in British waters, six months later, I jumped ship with all my pay and made my way to Liverpool. He was a decent man, Jack Philips; he gave me a job as a junior clerk, and sent me to evening classes to study bookkeeping. Later, I switched to an accountancy course. By the time I was twenty-one I had discovered a flair for investment and was making quite large sums of money. Then I studied law. Jack encouraged me to set my sights high—at the time my biggest dream was of a partnership with him, but by the time I was twenty-six I was in practice on my own as an accountant, and I had a very large investment portfolio. I met some wealthy and influential men during those years, including Harry Weiner, and eventually I was invited to join his merchant bank. At the time I never thought I would end up running an entire place of my own, of course.'

'It's like a fairy-story,' Emilie said breathlessly. 'I don't understand why you're so afraid of anyone finding out—people will admire you for fighting your way out of such a terrible childhood, they won't despise you for it. On the contrary.'

His eyes glowed with bitterness and a dark, burning anger. 'I know these men—they are very exclusive, they like to deal with men from their own world, not out-siders like me. None of them know I was born in Mexico, or know anything about my past. I've managed to ac-quire the right manner, the right voice, the right atti-tudes—they all assume I am one of them, but if they found I wasn't, they would turn on me.' He looked bleakly at her. 'So promise... Never tell anyone what I just told you. Even your grandfather.' He paused. 'And especially not Sophie. She would love to get her hands on a weapon to use against me.'

Emilie almost asked him why, but bit the words back. She remembered Sophie's black eyes glittering with hatred. He and Sophie had had an affair, he had ended it and Sophie was jealous—she hated seeing him with any other woman.

Poor Sophie, thought Emilie, I know how she feels, and was shaken to realise it was true—it made her sick to think of him with Sophie. But if I were her, I wouldn't want revenge because he had left me—I wouldn't want to destroy him. What good would that be?

'I can't believe anyone would be so cruel,' she protested, shaking her head.

'You don't know the world well enough yet,' Ambrose said gently. 'I know you find it hard to believe I'm right, but trust me.'

'I'd trust you with my life,' she said, and meant it.

He drew in breath, looked at her with darkened eyes. 'Thank you, Emilie.'

She had already trusted him with her heart, but he didn't know that. She wasn't as innocent as he thought she was, but he didn't know that either. I love him, she thought; and I want him to make love to me. I want it more than I have ever wanted anything else in my life.

CHAPTER SIX

SOPHIE and her mother spent Christmas at the house in Chelsea. Emilie had cooked a traditional meal of turkey, followed by a brandied Christmas pudding she had made months ago, which she served with brandy butter and cream.

Sophie came into the kitchen carrying two glasses of champagne. 'Merry Christmas, Emilie!' she said, offering her a glass.

'Merry Christmas!' Emilie took a sip of the wine; it felt dry and fizzy on her tongue, and made her sneeze.

'I thought someone else might join us ... Sholto Cory, maybe?' Sophie murmured, watching Emilie through her long black lashes. 'Or Ambrose?'

Emilie made a show of looking at the various pans bubbling away on the hob. 'Christmas is a family time, though, isn't it?' she said over her shoulder. 'Are you still seeing—what's his name? Gavin?'

'Gavin Wheeler,' Sophie said in an alert tone. 'Yes. Why?'

'I just wondered ... He works for Ambrose, doesn't he?'

'He's the secret of Ambrose's success.' Sophie's voice was acid. 'Ambrose is the façade, Gavin does all the work. He's a genius, in his own way; he can find out everything there is to know about a company in just a few days, turn it inside-out. He can smell hidden money and track down secrets that have been buried for years. Without him Ambrose wouldn't be where he is today.

But it's Ambrose who has the money and the power. This isn't a fair world.'

Emilie glanced at the book she had been reading, her eyes sombre. 'No, it isn't. But we're a lot better off in this country than people in some other countries.'

Sophie picked up the book. 'Mexico? I didn't know you liked travel books.'

Emilie went pink, suddenly realising the danger of talking about Mexico to Sophie. Ambrose didn't want her to know about his childhood.

'Oh...I...Yes...' she stammered, avoiding Sophie's curious gaze.

'Why are you looking so guilty?' probed Sophie, her eyes narrowing.

Emilie pretended to laugh. 'You're imagining things.'

George Rendell came into the kitchen at that moment. 'Anything I can do to help?'

'That was what I came in here to ask her,' Sophie said, smiling sweetly again.

'I can manage,' Emilie told them both, deeply relieved to change the subject. 'I must just check the dining-room.'

It gleamed with silver and crystal; Christmas crackers were beside each place, red candles in heavy Victorian silver candelabra in the centre of the table, and the room was full of the scent of white and dark red chrysanthemums with which the table was also decked.

Emilie served lunch dead on one o'clock; everything went perfectly, and afterwards they opened their Christmas presents around the tree. George Rendell had given Sophie a gold bracelet; her eyes lit up as she unwrapped it, slid it on to her slim wrist and held up her hand.

She kissed him on the cheek. 'Thank you, I love it.'

Aunt Rosa had been given a gold brooch: she seemed pleased with it and pinned it on her dress at once. Emilie wished she could be fond of her, but there was something so unreal about Aunt Rosa—she had had a face-lift and her smiles were always careful, as if she was afraid to stretch her skin too far. Her silvery hair had a blueish tint which suited her, but was very artificial.

George Rendell's parcel for Emilie held a blue suede box.

Emilie opened it, gasped, reverently lifted out a sapphire and diamond bracelet and held it up to the light to flash and sparkle with blue fire.

She heard Sophie's indrawn breath.

'Oh...' Emilie whispered. 'Grandpa...it's lovely...'

'It was your grandmother's; the stones are just the colour of her eyes—the colour of yours too.' He helped her fasten it around her wrist. Also in the box were matching earrings, fragile waterfalls of sapphires and diamonds which swung from her ears on silver thread and glittered every time she moved her head.

Sophie's eyes were as hard and glittering as the stones. She looked at them fixedly, her ripe red mouth parted with envy that was like a sort of hunger. 'Lucky girl,' she said icily.

She would love them, Emilie thought. This is what she would really have loved to be given—and was instantly uneasy, felt a pang of guilt because she had them and Sophie didn't. Emilie had never owned jewellery as expensive as this before. Although she loved the bracelet and earrings she would have been just as happy with anything her grandfather chose to give her. It was the love with which it was given that mattered to her.

'I hope they're insured,' Sophie said to George Rendell.

'Of course,' he said, gazing at her without expression. He had also noticed Sophie's eyes; he wasn't surprised. He had known Sophie for too long; he had had her measure years ago.

Later, Sophie and Emilie played cards while the older couple were resting. Sophie watched the flash of the sapphires and diamonds around Emilie's wrist as she dealt the cards.

'Have you any idea what they're worth?' Her voice was contemptuous.

'I don't care about that. I just love them because they were my grandmother's, and Grandpa gave them to me.'

The black eyes glittered furiously. 'He has never given me anything like that. But then, he's never liked me.'

'Oh, I'm sure he does!' Emilie protested, but remembered things her grandfather had said about Sophie and couldn't meet her eyes.

'He doesn't,' Sophie said bitingly. 'Just as well for you, isn't it? It made it so much easier for you to waltz in here and grab it all for yourself. With your big blue eyes and your sweet, innocent smile. The old man fell for it hook, line and sinker. He dotes on you; he'll leave you everything he's got. Well, you've fooled him, but you don't fool me.'

'I love my grandfather,' Emilie broke out, flushed and indignant. 'I'm not interested in his money.'

Sophie's mouth twisted. 'Well, you would say that, wouldn't you?'

Emilie looked at her sadly. There was no way she would ever convince Sophie that it was her grandfather's love she wanted, not his money.

Envy was a black root hidden deep inside the mind, twisting and spreading out of sight, poisoning everything it touched.

Sophie came up to her bedroom to wash and renew her make-up before she left. Emilie had forgotten that she had left another book on Mexico on her dressing-table; she had bought every book they had in the local bookshop. Sophie picked it up, flipped over the pages, and gave her another hard, thoughtful look.

'Are you planning a holiday in Mexico or something?'

Emilie shrugged, and said hurriedly, 'Maybe. Your mother's calling you...your taxi's here.'

Oh, why does life have to be so complicated? she thought as she and her grandfather waved goodbye to Sophie and her mother later.

'I told you those two would ruin Christmas,' George Rendell said, his eyes shrewd as they observed her.

'You hurt Sophie's feelings by giving me a much more expensive present,' Emilie told him, and he laughed angrily.

'You're my granddaughter—who had a better right to your grandmother's jewels?'

Envy isn't interested in explanations, thought Emilie; all Sophie knew was that *she* had what Sophie wanted. That was enough to make Sophie hate her.

The take-over began in the New Year. The office buzzed with rumour, uncertainty and dismay. Some of the staff had never worked anywhere else. They were afraid they were going to lose their jobs.

'New management always means sackings,' one of them said gloomily.

Emilie tried to reassure them, but she knew almost nothing of the plans Ambrose and the new managing director had for the mill.

George Rendell moved out of his office into a new one at the other end of the corridor the day before the new managing director arrived.

Stephen Hawdry was a man in his thirties, tall, thin, very serious, with brown hair and eyes and a rather shy manner when he talked to Emilie alone on the afternoon of his first day.

'I want to make it easy on your grandfather. I realise how hard this must be for him. He was very kind to me when I worked here.'

'I know he had a high opinion of you.'

Stephen smiled. 'That's nice. Are you happy where you are in the sales department? Because I thought it might please your grandfather if you started working with me—I have a secretary, of course, but being new to this job I could do with an assistant who knows everyone and who works here and can make my life easier.'

It was promotion and would undoubtedly please her grandfather. Emilie accepted the offer without needing to think about it, and moved into the office the following Monday.

She liked Stephen and found him easy to work for. She was grateful to him for the careful way he treated her grandfather too, with warmth and courtesy and sensitivity. He asked his advice, made sure George Rendell was fully informed of everything that happened, and he was friendly to Emilie too.

'He makes me feel I haven't been kicked out, so much as moved up!' Grandpa told her, ruefully smiling. 'He's a good lad, is Stephen.'

'I like him,' nodded Emilie. 'He likes me to be there when he sees members of staff so that I can fill him in with details of their private lives—if they have children, if they are getting married soon—and he never forgets what I've told him. Next time he sees them he doesn't need reminding who they are, where they live, how many children they've got. He's a very good manager.'

Ambrose called in several times that week to see how things were going. George might have warmed to Stephen Hawdry, but he was still prickly with Ambrose.

'What's he doing here again?' he asked, glaring as he saw Ambrose's Rolls drive into the car park. 'I can do without him peering over my shoulder all day.' He retreated back to his own office. Stephen was down on the shop-floor. Emilie was left alone to face Ambrose, her skin hot as she heard him walk into the room.

'Hello. I'm afraid Stephen is in the works.'

He nodded curtly. 'I'll go and find him in a minute. How are you enjoying working up here?'

'Very much.' Something in the glitter of his eyes made her very edgy.

'I drove past your place last night.'

Blankly she looked up at him. 'Oh?' Why was his tone so odd?

'I saw Sholto's car there.'

The blaze of his eyes made her nerves jump. Sholto kept calling on her, trying to persuade her to go out with him. He had come round last night and spent half an hour coaxing and pleading; Emilie didn't quite know how to handle it.

'I thought you weren't dating him!' Ambrose harshly said, his face tight, and she bit her lower lip.

'I'm not, but I don't know how to stop him coming to the house. I keep saying no, but he doesn't take any notice.'

'If you mean it, he'll get the message!' There was a scathing note in his voice, as if he didn't believe her.

'I do mean it!' she insisted. 'But he won't listen to me!'

'He'll listen to me,' Ambrose said through his teeth. 'I'll give him your message.'

Alarmed, she said, 'I couldn't... You might... Don't, please!' His powerful body and that hard, insistent face made him far too dangerous an opponent for poor Sholto. Sholto might try to fight him and Emilie was afraid of what might happen.

His mouth twisted and his eyes flashed. 'You mean you don't want me interfering in whatever game you're playing with Sholto?'

'I'm not playing games! But I can't send you to deal with Sholto for me—it would be so humiliating for him.'

He gave her an odd look. 'You're too soft-hearted. With guys like Sholto Cory you have to be tough.'

'I'm sure Sholto will realise I mean it, in the end.'

Ambrose turned to go, then looked round, his voice offhand. 'You told me you like ballet, didn't you? Are you free on Tuesday evening? I've got tickets for the first night of the new production of *Giselle*.'

The shock of the invitation left her so stunned that she only just managed to reply. 'Oh...thank you. I'd love to go,' she said, breathless.

'I'll pick you up at home, at six-thirty,' Ambrose said in the same curt, offhand manner.

When Emilie told her grandfather that Ambrose was taking her out, George Rendell frowned.

'Why on earth did you accept? He's far too old for you, and you can't trust him an inch.'

'It's only an evening at the ballet, Grandpa. I'll be safe enough!'

'Hmm...' said her grandfather, scowling.

Emilie bought a new dress for the occasion—cherry-red, a warm, soft jersey wool which clung smoothly to her figure.

When she came downstairs in it the following Tuesday evening her grandfather gave her another of those thoughtful, faintly uneasy looks.

'That's new, isn't it?'

'Don't you like it?'

He didn't have time to answer; there was a ring at the doorbell. 'That must be my taxi,' he said. He was going to have dinner with friends in Finchley. 'I'll be back around ten, I expect,' he told her. 'Don't be too late yourself. Make Ambrose bring you straight home.'

She waved goodbye, and was about to close the front door again when Sholto drove up. Emilie's heart sank.

'I'm going out in a minute, Sholto!'

'Who with? Or can I guess?' Flushed and angry, he eyed her insolently from head to foot, then whistled. 'You look sexy—does it feel as good as it looks?'

Before she could stop him he put out a hand to stroke the soft wool covering her shoulder.

'Don't!' she protested, shrugging his hand away.

He turned dark red, scowling. 'Do you say that to Ambrose? How far has he got?'

Hot colour ran up her face. 'I'm not even answering that!'

Sholto's mercurial temper flashed out of control again. 'Been to bed with him yet?'

She tried to get back into the house and slam the door on him, but he caught her and held her in spite of her struggles; he tried to kiss her mouth and when she turned her head away started kissing her neck. One of his hands strayed down over the red dress, found the warm swell of her breast and cupped it. He gave a groan.

'Oh, Em, stop seeing him . . . I know he's loaded, but he's old enough to be your father!'

At that moment Ambrose drove up and Emilie agitatedly said, 'There he is now! Let me go, Sholto!'

'I'm not scared of him,' muttered Sholto, but he released her and moved back. 'So you really are going out with him?' His mouth writhed in jealousy and fury. 'How can you, Em?'

Angrily, he walked off, got into his own car, started the engine and drove off with a squeal of tyres.

Emilie felt her heart kick over as Ambrose came towards her, a tall, shadowy figure in the darkness, his black hair blowing back from his forehead, his coat collar turned up against a bitter winter wind.

'I've just got to set the burglar-alarm—I won't be a minute!' she said breathlessly, collecting her coat and gloves and putting them on.

He watched her as she switched on the alarm and set the special locks on the front door before closing it behind them.

'Isn't there anyone else in the house?' he asked in a curt, hard voice.

'No, Grandpa has gone out to dinner.'

His next question was shot at her like a bullet from a revolver. 'So you were alone here with young Cory?'

She felt her nerves jump, and hurriedly said, 'He only arrived just as Grandpa left.'

His face was like a clenched fist; she felt the threat of it as if it were a physical one.

'How long ago was that? What have the two of you been doing ever since?'

'Nothing!' She was pale, alarmed by his glittering eyes, the tension of face and voice. This was an Ambrose she had never seen before. He frightened her.

'Nothing?' he repeated, biting the word out between his teeth. 'Don't lie to me! I saw you in his arms as I drove up.' His scathing stare ran down over her body, lingered on her breasts.

'Then you must have seen me trying to push him away!'

His mouth twisted cynically. 'Oh, yes—when you saw me drive up!'

'No, Ambrose! Why should I lie about it? And stop shouting at me, I don't like it!'

He stared at her, his black brows together, the anger slowly dying out of his face, then grimaced. 'Was I shouting? Sorry. You should have let me deal with Sholto weeks ago. Well, never mind. Let's go, shall we?'

As they drove he told her that he had booked a table for supper after the ballet at one of London's fashionable restaurants.

The ballet was magical: visually beautiful and poignant, leaving Emilie with a lump in her throat. They came out still in a trance of enchantment to find London white with snow. While they were in the theatre a blizzard had blown out of nowhere; the streets were half-empty and cars were inching along slowly, skidding on the icy roads.

'I think we had better skip supper and get you home at once,' Ambrose said reluctantly as they got into his car.

She didn't argue, although she was very disappointed; she could see he was right. The snow was thickening, if anything, and above them the sky sagged like a great grey quilt, heavy with yet more snow.

As they carefully joined the traffic crawling along the Embankment Emilie asked him, 'Will your housekeeper be up to make you a quick meal?'

'No, but I can make myself a sandwich, or find some smoked salmon in the fridge!' He was staring through the windscreen, his eyes narrowed in an effort to see the road through the constantly drifting snow which was falling across the glass. The windscreen-wipers couldn't cope; they kept getting stuck.

It took them an age to reach her home. Emilie gave him an uncertain look before getting out of the car. 'I shall make myself a light snack—just scrambled eggs, an omelette maybe, something like that. You're very welcome to come in and share it.'

His grey eyes were hooded, watching her through dark lashes. 'Won't your grandfather object to visitors at this hour of the night?'

'He won't mind, and anyway, he's probably in bed asleep by now!'

'Well, if you're sure it isn't too much trouble... Thanks, I'd love to share your supper.'

They hurried to the front door, unlocked it and shut the wind out before too much snow blew into the house. Emilie turned off the burglar-alarm while Ambrose was stamping his snowy shoes on the doormat.

'Can I take your coat?' Emilie held out her hand for it, noticing that even his eyelashes had snow on them.

He took off his coat, long scarf and leather gloves, and handed them to her. She put them all into the Victorian hall wardrobe and hung up her own coat beside his, frowning suddenly.

'What's wrong?' Ambrose asked.

'My grandfather's coat should be here, but it isn't.' A pang of alarm hit her—she began to imagine the worst scenarios. In weather like this anything might have happened; so easy for a car to crash on a busy motorway in a blizzard. Her grandfather was an old man, frail;

even if he wasn't seriously injured the shock of an accident could threaten his life.

'He has probably been delayed by the snow,' Ambrose reassured her. 'Do you have the phone number of his friends?'

She shook her head.

'What's their name? We can ask Directory Enquiries for the number.'

'Brown,' she said ruefully, and he grimaced.

'Ah. Do you know where they live?'

'Finchley.'

'What's the name of the road?'

'I've no idea.'

Ambrose considered her wryly. 'Has your grandfather got an address-book?'

'Yes, but I'm not sure where he keeps it, and I wouldn't like to search his desk.' She paused, sighed. 'Not yet, anyway.' She frowned at her watch. 'I'll cook our supper. Maybe he'll be here by then.'

'Can I help? I enjoy watching you cook.'

Her skin flowered with colour, and she hurried off to the kitchen with Ambrose at her heels. He glanced curiously around the large, Victorian room. It had a high ceiling, from which hung an original wooden laundry rack which was used now to display dried flowers—lavender, roses, herbs, which scented the air—and a string of French onions.

'What can I do to help?' he asked.

'Could you lay the table? We'll eat in here; it's warmer and easier at this time of night.' She showed him where the cutlery was kept, then took eggs from a dish on the old Welsh dresser, beating them up in a blue and white china bowl while Ambrose was laying the pine table in the centre of the kitchen.

Glancing at him, Emilie asked, 'Do you want a plain omelette, or shall I add something? Herbs, cheese, tomato, ham, or mushrooms? What would you like?'

'Herbs, and just a little cheese?'

She grated cheese, sliced bread, made a pot of coffee, then heated butter in a pan on the old Aga range which sat in an alcove. Emilie beat some herbs into the eggs and poured the mixture into the pan, began to draw a fork through the cooking egg, and while it was still soft added the grated cheese. When it was ready she flipped it over into a perfect golden semicircle on to one of the warmed plates, then divided the omelette into two.

'I'm starving,' Ambrose confessed as he sat down at the table. 'The smell of the food is making my mouth water.' He forked omelette into his mouth, tasted it, closed his eyes and sighed. 'You are such a good cook! This is the best omelette I've ever eaten.'

'Omelettes are easy.'

'Then why is that so many of the omelettes I've eaten appeared to be made of rubber?' he drawled, making her laugh.

Emilie poured coffee and they carried it through into the sitting-room once they had eaten. They talked for ten minutes, drinking the coffee, then Ambrose said he must be on his way.

As they were leaving the room Emilie suddenly noticed a little red light flashing on the telephone.

'A message from your grandfather?' guessed Ambrose.

He was right. George Rendell had rung just before they themselves got back. 'Emilie, it's ten-thirty, and snowing so hard here that I don't think I should risk the drive back in the dark. Mona and Fred have offered me a bed for the night.'

She drew a nervous breath and Ambrose gave her a quick, searching look.

George Rendell's message went on, 'I'll be back in the morning. I'm sorry to leave you alone in the house at night. If you're nervous, give Sophie a ring. I'm sure she'll come over to stay with you.'

Emilie gave a sigh of mingled relief and dismay. She was glad to know what had happened to her grandfather, and be sure he was safe, but she was not too keen on being alone in the house at night, and did not want Sophie's company.

Ambrose was watching her, his brows together. 'Nervous about being alone?'

'I'll be fine,' she lied, forcing a smile.

He looked at his watch. 'You'd better ring Sophie at once.'

'I don't want Sophie here!'

His eyes narrowed, searching her flushed and angry face. 'I thought you were fond of Sophie. What's changed? Has she upset you? What has she said to you?'

'Nothing,' she said. She didn't want to talk about what had happened at Christmas; Sophie's bitter envy of her over her grandmother's jewels, the barbed remarks Sophie had made about him. 'Did you ever tell Sophie what you told me?' she asked hesitantly.

He looked blank. 'What do you mean?'

'About your childhood.'

His face changed, hardened. 'No, I certainly did not! And she's the last person I'd want to know,' he muttered, frowning. 'Don't forget, you promised never to tell anyone, especially Sophie!'

'I haven't forgotten!' she protested. 'I wouldn't.'

The silence stretched between them again, quivering, as fragile as a cobweb, and as sharp and glittering as a sword.

'I'm sorry,' Ambrose said huskily, touching her cheek with one long index finger. 'Don't look so frightened. I didn't mean to snap.'

Her lashes down, she quivered, her heart beating far too fast.

His finger stroked her mouth and it parted; she was breathing as if she had been running.

Ambrose bent down closer, she closed her eyes and lifted her mouth, his lips touched it—and at that second there was a loud crash upstairs.

They jumped apart.

'What was that?' gasped Emilie.

'I thought the house was empty?' Ambrose was quicker-witted than she was; he was already on his way into the hall.

'It is! I mean . . . it should be.' A pulse of anxiety beat in her throat as she followed him.

They stood at the bottom of the stairs. There were other sounds now; she couldn't make out what they were.

'Something or someone is moving up there,' Ambrose told her. 'I'll investigate—you stay here.'

'Shouldn't I ring the police?'

'Not yet. It might be a bird that has flown down a chimney in the storm. If you hear me shout, ring then.'

As he began to creep up the stairs, she whispered after him, 'Please be careful!'

He vanished, swallowed up by the darkness at the top of the stairs.

She waited, agitated, pale, listening intently, and eventually heard a muffled cry—had that been his signal?

She turned to run to the phone, to ring the police. Before she got there, the lights came on upstairs, dazzling her. Emilie swung round again. Ambrose was coming back down the stairs two at a time.

'What was it?' she gasped.

'A burglar. He got away,' he said grimly. 'I just got a glimpse of him climbing down the fire-escape next door. He'd tried to come down through the skylight in the roof, but the wooden frame must have been rotten. It broke—that was the crash we heard. There's glass all over the floor in the little bedroom at the top of the house.'

'We'd better ring the police—he might come back!'

'Oh, we must ring them—though I doubt if he'll be back, at least tonight—but I think he might have hurt himself. There was blood on the glass.'

She gave a cry of dismay. 'Did he fall down through the glass?'

'I think he half fell through, but managed to drag himself back up on to the roof, then slid down the roof-tiles to the fire-escape next door.'

Ambrose strode past her to pick up the phone and dial the emergency services, asking for the police.

Emilie poured them both more coffee and sat down, nursing her own cup in both hands, feeling very cold, listening as Ambrose told the police what had happened.

'I only saw him for a second,' he explained. 'Small, skinny chap, in a balaclava helmet and black tracksuit—he must be freezing in this weather, dressed like that. No topcoat or jacket, either. No, he didn't get anything. I think he may be injured—there was blood on the broken glass. But he might try again somewhere else in this neighbourhood.'

He listened, nodding. 'Very well, we won't touch anything. Luckily there's a lock on the door—I'll make sure that if he does come back he can't get into the house from that room. I've already locked the door. I'll barricade it with a heavy piece of furniture too.'

He paused, listened again, then said, 'OK, tomorrow, then.' He hung up and looked at her wryly. 'The police don't feel it is urgent enough to warrant a visit tonight. They'll come tomorrow to take samples of the blood and fingerprints, if there are any—so we aren't to touch anything in that room.'

'I heard you tell him you'd already locked the door.' She was very pale. 'Maybe I should ring Sophie, after all,' she thought aloud. Then she looked at her watch. 'It's nearly midnight! I can't ring her at this hour!'

Yet she was worried by the idea of spending the night in this house alone now.

Coolly, Ambrose said, 'No need to disturb Sophie—I'll stay. I think it would be best for there to be a man in the house. Just in case our friend comes back.'

'Do you think he might?'

He caught the flash of alarm in her eyes and quickly added, 'No, I'm sure he won't. But better to be safe than sorry. I can sleep on the couch down here. All I need is a blanket or a quilt and a pillow.'

'There are plenty of spare rooms; we can quickly make up a bed. If you're sure you don't mind. I must admit, I'd sleep easier if I knew I wasn't alone in the house.'

'And I wouldn't sleep at all if I thought you were alone here,' Ambrose drily told her.

She blushed.

They went upstairs and she showed him to the best spare bedroom. It was large and comfortably furnished; they made up the bed together and Emilie found him a towelling robe and a pair of her grandfather's striped pyjamas.

'I don't suppose they'll fit too well.' He was so much taller than her grandfather, longer in the leg, broader in the shoulder, deeper in the chest.

'I don't wear anything to bed,' he calmly said.

'Oh,' she said, eyes enormous, shimmering.

Ambrose looked into them. 'Goodnight, Emilie,' he murmured, his voice husky.

'Goodnight,' she whispered and almost fled to her room.

She stood by the window looking out at the whirling snow before she drew the curtains. Her mind was whirling too, with images that made her feel faint.

Ambrose was in the room right next door to her. They were alone together in this house.

Her heart beat so hard she felt it might burst right through her ribcage.

Outside, the sound of London was deadened by the snow. All the usual noises seemed to have ceased, or to be muffled: traffic passing along the Embankment, the running of the river, the wailing of police and ambulances speeding around the city, the hoarse wail of ship foghorns. She couldn't hear anything but the whine of the wind.

Drawing the curtains with a shiver, she turned to start undressing. Was that what Ambrose was doing too? She let her silky slip slide to the floor and took off her bra, staring at her reflection in the dressing-table mirror: the full, soft milky flesh of her breasts, the aroused hardness of her nipples, the long, bare legs and the curly dark hair in that triangle between them.

What did Ambrose look like naked? He was tall, very fit; even in his elegant city suits you could glimpse the muscled power of the body underneath. Her mouth dried. She closed her eyes, imagining him naked.

What would it be like if...?

Her mind whirled even more, conjuring up those images of him, naked, his broad shoulders and deep chest, his long-fingered hands touching her, his mouth...

She suddenly remembered Sholto, earlier, touching her, kissing her neck.

It hadn't done a thing for her, except to make her want to hit Sholto.

If it had been Ambrose touching her, though... She groaned, imagining his hand on her breast, his mouth moving against her throat, his thigh pushing between her own.

I'm out of my mind! she told herself. I must stop thinking about him.

She picked up the white Victorian nightie she meant to wear. It was one of the Christmas presents her grandfather had given her—starched cotton, floor-length, long-sleeved, buttoned to the neck, with broderie anglaise on the ruffled bodice. He had said his mother had worn one just like it—'Is it too old-fashioned?' he had asked uncertainly.

'I love it,' Emilie had said, loving the delicate embroidery, the demure look of it.

When she had cleaned her face and brushed her teeth, she climbed into bed and snuggled down under her duvet with a grateful sigh.

Was Ambrose in bed too? Was he already asleep? She mustn't start thinking about him again, or she would never get to sleep.

She closed her eyes, and then they flew open in shock as she heard another crash and splintering of glass from the floor above.

Emilie was out of bed in a flash, running to the door.

As she shot out on to the landing she almost collided with Ambrose, who seemed to be wearing only her grandfather's black- and red-striped towelling robe.

'Did you hear it?' she gasped.

'Yes. Stay here,' he ordered curtly, and made for the narrow flight of stairs that led to the upper floor.

Shivering, Emilie waited; she heard him dragging aside the heavy chest he had earlier pushed in front of the door of the room which the burglar had fallen into before.

A moment later he came back towards her. 'It's OK, he hadn't come back—what we heard was the last of the broken skylight crashing into the room, brought down by the weight of snow which had settled on the glass.'

'Oh,' she breathed, very relieved. 'Thank heavens you were here! I don't know what I would have done if I'd been here on my own!'

He looked down at her, frowning. 'You're shivering. You'd better get straight back to bed.' He put an arm round her shoulders to turn her and lead her back into her bedroom.

She was so aware of his bare legs and feet that she stumbled over the long folds of her nightie.

Ambrose tightened his grip to stop her falling, then suddenly swept her right off her feet, lifting her up into his arms.

Startled, she clutched at him, her heart banging like a drum. He began to walk towards the bed; she tentatively slid her arms around his neck, sinking against him, her head on his chest, very conscious that it was bare where the towelling robe parted at the lapels.

Ambrose began to lower her to the bed. She went on clinging, her body soft and pliant in his arms.

Ambrose made a muffled sound in his throat; he sat down on the edge of the bed, still holding her. His head came down and hers lifted. Their mouths met with a rush, an explosion of need and feeling; heat broke out between them instantly.

He groaned her name. 'Emilie!'

The sound made the hairs on the back of her neck stand up. His voice had such hunger in it.

She had never been kissed like this—it was an invasion, so intimate that she was shocked, and yet she was excited by the probing of his tongue into the moist inner warmth of her mouth, the demanding movement of his lips.

The kiss had a disturbing effect on her; she seemed to be boneless, she was melting, like hot wax. His hands moved sensuously on her nightdress, the starched folds of white cotton, moulding them to her like a sculptor creating a woman from clay, her body emerging under his touch: her high, firm breasts, her small waist, the soft curve of hip and thigh.

She was trembling, eyes tightly shut, as she caressed his black hair, the nape of his neck, her fingers sliding inside the robe, the small dark hairs roughening his naked chest prickling under her fingertips.

That was how she found the sickle-shaped scar, a raised contour she could feel. She lay still, tracing it, remembering what he had told her about the man who had tried to kill him when he was a boy.

Ambrose quietly said, 'Yes, that's the knife-scar.'

She shivered. 'An inch or two to the side and it would have gone into your heart.'

'It was meant to. I was lucky.'

'It must have hurt badly.' There were tears under her lids. 'Poor little boy.' She could almost see him then, a thin, ragged child with blood seeping through his torn shirt. She kissed the scar softly. 'I wish I'd been there to take care of you.'

Ambrose stroked her hair. 'I'd have had to take care of you,' he drily said, but his voice was moved. 'You're very sweet, Emilie.'

She burrowed into him like a small animal seeking refuge, her nostrils quivering at the scent of him, her head heavy as it fell against his powerful chest, her mouth parting, her tongue tasting the saltiness of his skin, the roughness of the curved scar.

She heard his faint groan. 'Do you know what you're doing?'

'Yes.' She knew. She was doing what she had wanted to do for a long time, what she had fantasised about earlier, in this room, looking at herself naked in the mirror and imagining him naked. She had daydreamed about seeing him, touching him, having him touch her— was this just another daydream? Or was it really happening?

He breathed thickly as her hands moved downwards, following the hard, flat planes of his body; they tangled in the rough bush of hair between his thighs. He gave a sharp moan. 'Emilie. God, you're driving me crazy. Emilie . . . I want you, God knows, but you're so young.'

Her pulses beat wildly. He wanted her. He wanted her. She looked up at him through lowered lashes and saw his face; she barely recognised it now—it was strange, unfamiliar, disturbing.

His skin was darkly flushed, over a bone-structure which had become a taut mask. His eyes were so hot she felt as if they might burn her. His lips were apart; he breathed through them roughly, unsteadily.

'It wouldn't be fair to you; you'll regret this in the morning,' he grated, frowning.

He tried to unlock her arms, push her away against the pillows, but she held him, her body arching in invitation.

'Don't go... Don't leave me...' she whispered, and heard his breath catch, heard him give another deep, hoarse groan.

'You don't know what you're saying.'

'Of course I do,' she said almost angrily, husky, very flushed. 'I'm not a child, I'm a woman.'

Her mouth found his; she kissed him passionately, and she felt Ambrose shuddering, then he began to kiss her back hard, his mouth hungry, demanding. Emilie sank backwards, taking him with her, their bodies tangling on the bed. He was heavy. Driven by instinct as old as time, she moved under him, her legs parting so that he sank between them, her nightdress riding up so that their bare skin touched.

Ambrose broke off the kiss, sat up, shrugged out of his robe, and she looked at him, swallowing, so hot that she felt feverish.

He was naked now, as she had imagined him; her stare moved slowly down over the powerful chest, the lean hips, the dark tangle of hair between his long, slim legs.

Ambrose was watching her, breathing as if he were drowning.

Hoarsely, he said, 'Listen... I can't do this... You're a virgin, aren't you, Emilie?'

She hesitated. If she said she was he might stop making love to her; but if she lied he would soon find out. How could she hide the fact that she had never made love before?

'You are, aren't you?' His eyes were unreadable, the pupils glazed, enlarged, very black. She could hear the rough drag of his breathing.

She groaned. 'Yes, but... I want you. I want you to be the first... don't you see?'

'Will you marry me?'

It was the last thing she had expected him to say.

For a moment she was too stunned to say anything. Her voice when it came was trembling. 'Oh...yes...yes, Ambrose, yes.'

He bent his head and kissed her deeply. 'Now you belong to me,' he told her. 'I'll make you happy, Emilie, I'll take great care of you. But I hope you're absolutely sure about this, because once we are married I'll never let you go. I'm a very possessive man—never make me jealous, or you'll wish you had never been born.'

'I've never been more certain of anything in my life!' she protested. 'I'd never even look at another man!'

'I'd kill you if you did,' he said, his eyes dark, and she felt a stab of fear.

He was deadly serious, and it scared her, but she knew she would never feel this way about anyone else, so she pushed the thought away, pulling him back down towards her, her hands trembling, eager.

'You don't need to have any doubts about me. I love you. All I want is to belong to you.'

His voice was deep, rough. 'All right, Emilie. You're going to!'

He was gentle, but it hurt; her body tensed involuntarily, resisting him, refusing to yield to the hard, naked flesh attempting to enter it.

'I'm hurting you... I don't want to hurt you,' Ambrose said, trying to withdraw, but her arms tightened round his back, pulling him down. She wrapped her legs around him too, enclosing him in her body.

'I don't care... Hurt me, I want you to,' she groaned.

'Emilie,' he said, sounding shaken, almost shocked. 'Well, if you're sure... But stop me if it hurts too much.'

And then he finally took her—his body entering her with a force that was like dying. She bit back the cry of pain she couldn't help, swallowed it into herself, trying to relax her clenched muscles.

Ambrose sighed heavily, lay still inside her for a moment. 'It will be easier next time,' he whispered. 'I'll be as gentle as I can.'

He began to move, slowly, softly; each movement hurt. Emilie felt faint, but the pain was nothing compared with the fact that Ambrose was inside her, they were part of each other. She closed her eyes and clung to him, abandoning herself, her body totally submissive.

Ambrose slowly lost control. He groaned; his thrusts grew deeper, deeper, until he was driving fiercely into her, his hot face between her breasts, his cries of pleasure and satisfaction so loud that he was unaware that she was silent.

Afterwards he fell forward on her and lay there, breathing hoarsely, roughly.

Emilie held him in her arms, hearing his breathing slow, feeling his shuddering body quieten and lie still.

Their bodies entwined, naked and silky; they lay in drowsy silence, heavy with the peace that came after such rending passion, warm with the onset of sleep.

When they fell asleep it was like drowning in a deep, dark sea. Emilie kept dreaming of him; over and over again he took her, and in her dream she experienced the quivering, shuddering pleasure she had not felt when she was awake, her body clamouring and moist, open to him as a sea-anemone, drawing him in and keeping him. Over and over again.

CHAPTER SEVEN

AMBROSE woke up first. Emilie drowsily felt movement in the bed beside her, a smothered groan, then the springs of the bed gave as Ambrose leapt out.

For a second she thought she was dreaming, then with a rush memory came back. She went scarlet. Her mind flooded with pictures. Oh, how could I? she thought, remembering herself begging him not to go, to stay with her, winding her arms around his neck and holding him back when he tried to leave.

Ambrose stood there looking down at her; she felt him watching her and pretended sleep.

At last he moved away. Warily, she lifted her lids a fraction, peered through the slit; saw him, naked, at the bedroom door, and her heart missed a beat.

She had wondered what he looked like naked. Now she knew.

His back was smooth, still with the remnants of a summer tan; as he moved, the muscles under the silky skin rippled. You would never suspect he was more than thirty; he had an amazingly fit, athletic body. She knew he walked a good deal, worked out at a gym several times a week, usually had a swim too.

Her eyes explored his rear view obsessively, noticing everything: the deep indentation running down the spine, the firm buttocks, the long, slim legs, their calves roughened by tiny black hairs.

The bedroom door closed behind him. Emilie jumped out of bed, realising how cold it still was—the central heating wasn't yet on and the house was icy.

Shivering, she bolted her bedroom door, showered, got dressed, did her hair and make-up, moving like a robot, her mind too busy with what had happened last night to think about anything else. He'd asked her to marry him—had he meant it?

Why would he say it if he didn't mean it? she defiantly asked herself, and knew the answer to that.

Because he had felt guilty about what he wanted to do? Ambrose had a conscience. She had been a virgin, and still very young, the granddaughter of a friend. Had he felt he couldn't seduce her without promising to marry her?

He meant it, I'm sure he meant it! her heart said, and her head coolly answered, Oh, maybe last night he meant it at the time—but would he remember it this morning?

She heard a car in the street outside and tensed—was that her grandfather coming back?

She ran to the window to look out. The street was oddly different this morning—the rooftops coated with hard snow, icicles hanging from drainpipes, bushes and trees dusted with white. A car slowly drove past and vanished. She sagged in relief for a second, then thought, What if her grandfather *had* come back?

She shuddered at the thought of his face if he had walked into that room and found them naked in bed together. She'd have wanted to die.

A knock on her bedroom door made her jump, then freeze.

'Emilie?'

'Yes?' She was so nervous her voice trembled. Although she was fully dressed she didn't move to open the door. She was afraid of facing him. How was he going to look at her now?

'It's seven-thirty. I have to go—I've got a busy day ahead of me.' A pause, then he said quickly, 'Are you OK?'

'Yes,' she whispered.

'You sound shy again,' he said, and his voice held a smile. 'I hate to leave you, but I have to get some work done! You're coming between me and my job, Emilie. I'll be back tonight, to talk to your grandfather. I'll come at seven—we'll have dinner somewhere special. I'll book for three. You can tell your grandfather we're engaged, or wait until I get here if you'd rather I broke the news.' He paused, then said softly, 'Wear the blue dress you wore the night we first met, at my Christmas party. I love you in that.'

She heard him walking away, his footsteps on the creaking wooden stairs. The front door opened and closed, his car door slammed, the engine started, there was a roar of acceleration and the car drove off.

He had meant it. He was going to tell her grandfather he wanted to marry her. She felt a rush of happiness— she was so light she almost felt she could float. She put her palms against her flushed cheeks, staring at herself in the mirror.

He loved her. He must love her. Why else would he want to marry her?

She searched her face incredulously—why me? Of all the women in the world Ambrose could marry... why her? Why not someone like Sophie—someone sophisticated, elegant, worldly-wise?

Her mouth went crooked. If she was surprised, what was everyone else going to think? Sophie... She winced at the thought of Sophie's reaction.

Sophie had envied her that bracelet, those earrings, envied her because she thought she might one day inherit Grandpa's money! But those had just been material things Sophie coveted. Ambrose was far more important. Emilie was certain Sophie had been in love with him, was still sexually obsessed with Ambrose.

She'll hate me! Emilie shivered at the thought.

And what about Grandpa? What was he going to think? No, she couldn't possibly break it to Grandpa; she would leave that to Ambrose.

She heard a taxi pull up outside... the chugging note of the engine unmistakable. Only a London taxi sounded like that. She ran to the window to look out again at the wintry street. This time it really was her grandfather; he got out, paid the driver, made his way with great care over the icy pavement.

She ran downstairs and met him in the hall. 'Are you all right?' they asked each other almost in harmony, then both laughed.

'I'm fine,' he said. 'The snow is still hanging about in the streets, but it isn't so cold this morning.'

'Have you had breakfast?'

'I had coffee and a slice of toast with Fred and Mona. Did you get Sophie to stay with you?'

'No, I didn't, but...something did happen last night,' she said, hesitating. She had to break the news of the attempted burglary; he had to be told about that.

He listened, horrified. 'You say the police didn't even come?'

'Well, nothing had been stolen and the burglar had got away.'

Turning dark red, George Rendell stamped over to the phone and rang the local police station, complained angrily, demanded someone come round to the house at once so that he could get the skylight replaced as soon as possible.

Mary arrived to clean the house as he put the phone down. Emilie told her about the break-in, and warned her not to enter the little box-room at the top of the house.

'The police are coming this morning,' George Rendell told them. 'Mary, you'll be here, won't you, all day? Ring the builder who did some work for me last year. Once the police have seen the roof and got their finger-prints and so on, the skylight can be replaced, I expect. Better check with the police that that will be OK.' He looked at his watch, frowning. 'We'll have to go. It's getting late.'

Emilie anxiously asked, 'Should you drive, in this weather? Maybe we should get a taxi?'

'All the way to Kent? Certainly not. The main roads will have been cleared by now.'

As they walked to the garage, George Rendell said, 'Lucky Ambrose was still here when it happened.'

A chill ran down her spine. Now it would start—his questions, speculation. Trying to be casual, she shrugged. 'Yes, it was very lucky. If I'd been alone I'd have been scared stiff.'

'I still don't understand why you didn't ring Sophie...especially after someone tried to break in like that. You shouldn't have spent the night in the house alone.'

'I didn't,' she said huskily, not meeting his eyes. 'Ambrose stayed.'

George Rendell skidded on the snowy path, almost fell over, and grabbed at her arm to save himself, swearing under his breath.

'What do you mean? Stayed all night?' he hoarsely asked.

'In one of the spare rooms,' she whispered.

Her grandfather stared fixedly. 'You should have rung me!'

'I would have, if I'd had a phone number for your friends! But all I knew was their surname—and there are lots of Browns in London.'

'In future I'll make sure I leave a number where I can be reached!' he muttered as they entered the garage and got into the car. 'All right, you couldn't ring me—but why didn't you ring Sophie?'

'Sophie and I don't get on very well lately.'

Her grandfather started the engine, scowling. 'What does that mean? Why don't you? I thought you were friends.'

'I thought we were, but... Well, ever since Christmas I've realised that Sophie doesn't like me; she's jealous. She was angry because you gave me Grandma's sapphire bracelet and earrings. She wanted them, and she was bitter about it.'

The car moved slowly down the street and turned into the Embankment, which had been sanded and was already clear of snow as the volume of traffic melted it. George Rendell stared ahead, frowning while he thought over what Emilie had said.

'I did warn you what she was like,' he said heavily. 'I'm sorry you've been disillusioned, dear. Even so, you should have got her over here for the night. You shouldn't have allowed Ambrose to stay when there was no one else in the house.' George Rendell stopped at traffic-lights and stared at the red light, drumming his fingers on the steering-wheel. There was silence for a moment, then he broke out, 'Merciful heavens, Emilie, don't you know what people would make of it?'

She was crimson. 'This is nearly the twenty-first century! Grandpa, Queen Victoria is dead! Who cares?'

He gave her a pitying, irritated look. 'The Press would eat up the story if it got out! Ambrose runs a respected city institution and he's seriously rich. The Press of this country is envy-motivated, like so many of their readers; anyone successful is a target for them. They'd love to pull Ambrose down—they'd leap at a chance to dig up a scandal about him to splash on their front pages. Sex and money sell newspapers.'

Emilie was upset, worried; she hated to see her grandfather in this state, but she was helpless to soothe him down because she couldn't tell him nothing had happened. She couldn't lie to him, except by omission.

Desperately, she told him, 'Ambrose said he would come over at seven and take us out to dinner.'

George Rendell turned his head to stare at her, his brows together. 'Dinner? Why?'

'He... he wants to talk to you, he said.'

The lights changed, and they drove off. Frowning, her grandfather asked, 'Talk to me about what? Business? No, he'd ring me at work. I suppose he wants to reassure me that you were safe with him in the house all night. Well, he doesn't need to tell me that. I know you, I'm sure nothing happened—but if it gets out, the Press will think the worst. They always do. Ambrose knows that, he knew very well what risk he was running, not just for himself—I don't give a damn about him—but for you. Your reputation could be ruined if this got out.'

They drove in silence; she was relieved when they reached the mill. Her grandfather went into the works to talk to someone, and she made her way to the managing director's office.

His secretary, Jill, looked up, smiled and said, 'Stephen just rang to say he has flu and is staying in bed today, he'll probably be off until Monday.'

'Oh, poor Stephen! Was there much for him to do today? My grandfather is in the works—he can cope with anything urgent.'

'Nothing much on.' Jill shrugged, looking at Stephen's diary.

Emilie sat down at her own desk in the little office next door. It just had room for her desk and chair and a filing-cabinet. The high windows looked out over the town, filtering grey winter light into the high-ceilinged room. She could hear the machinery of the mill, which was housed next door, in the oldest part of the building. A narrow stream ran beside the outer wall; when it was built the mill had operated on water power. Now it was electrically operated.

Her grandfather put his head round the door. 'I just heard about Stephen. I hope we aren't all going to get flu. It's going through the works; a dozen people are off sick this morning. I'll be next door if you want me. I'm taking over while Stephen is away.' Being needed had made him very cheerful; he grinned at her as he vanished.

The day dragged by; Emilie couldn't concentrate on her work because her mind was entirely full of Ambrose. It seemed an eternity before she was back in the car, heading home towards London.

'What time did you say Ambrose was coming?' her grandfather asked as they reached Chelsea.

'Seven. He said something about taking us out to dinner.'

'Hmm.'

George Rendell drove into his garage and they walked through into the house. There was a note from Mary on the kitchen table, telling them that the police had come, had said it was OK to have the damaged skylight replaced, and the builder had done the work already.

'Well, thank heavens for that!' George Rendell said.

'I must change,' Emilie said, running upstairs. She had a quick shower, then put on the pansy-blue silk Ambrose had asked her to wear.

She was about to come down when she heard the doorbell, then her grandfather's voice, followed by familiar deep, assured tones.

'Come in, Ambrose.'

'My shoes are covered with snow, I'm afraid.'

'Doesn't matter, come in out of this wind. Bitter again tonight, isn't it? Going to be black ice on the roads later. Emilie's upstairs changing. Care for a drink while we wait for her?'

They vanished into the sitting-room. She crept down the stairs and stood in the hall, trying to hear what they were saying. Ambrose's voice was quiet, calm.

Suddenly her grandfather's voice roared angrily. 'Damned stupid thing to do! She's as innocent as a newborn babe—no idea at all how it might look! But you're street-wise, Ambrose, you knew! You should have made her ring Sophie.'

'I might have done, George, if I hadn't asked her to marry me last night,' Ambrose said.

The silence was deafening.

'Good God,' George Rendell said at last, sounding as if someone had punched him in the stomach.

'I realise you may have reservations about that, but——'

'Reservations? For heaven's sake, man, she's half your age!'

'I know that, but if we love each other——'

'She hasn't had a chance to find out what love means! She's barely out of school, she's never had a boyfriend, unless you count Sholto Cory, and she only went out with him a few times.'

'He meant nothing!' Ambrose said curtly.

'He was besotted with her, and if you hadn't come between them it might have become serious! Emilie is still a child.'

'She's a woman and she knows what she wants.'

George Rendell's voice thickened into rage, distaste. 'What does that mean? What the hell's been going on behind my back? My God, you bastard, have you...?'

Emilie hated the sound of his voice, the violence of the tone, the words. She pushed open the door and both men were silent, stiffening, looking round at her.

Tears in her eyes, she pleaded, 'Please stop it. You mustn't fight. I love you both, I don't want you to quarrel, especially over me.'

Her grandfather was pale, his face carved with lines of distress and anger. He stared at her as if he didn't know her, had never seen her before.

Ambrose put out his hand and she ran to take it. He put his other arm round her possessively, turned his eyes to her grandfather.

'We want your blessing, George, but whether you approve or not, we are going to be married. She's of age. She doesn't need your consent.'

'I'm going to be happy, Grandpa,' Emilie quickly said, seeing her grandfather's face pale with fury. 'You'll see. I know you're upset, but the difference in age isn't as important as you think it is. What matters is that we love each other and we want to be together.'

'She'll be safe with me,' Ambrose said, and George Rendell gave him a level stare, his chin belligerent.

'If you don't make her happy, I'll kill you, Ambrose!'

The announcement was in *The Times* on a Saturday morning. Emilie hadn't told anyone and was relieved not to be going to work. It would give people a chance to get over the first surprise before she had to face their stares and curious questions.

What she hadn't anticipated was the phone calls. The phone began ringing just after breakfast.

Her grandfather took the first call, was politely curt with the caller, put the phone down and looked at her with a wry expression.

'Some gossip-columnist wanting to talk to you. I told her to get in touch with Ambrose's personal PR.'

'Has he got one?' There was still so much she didn't know about Ambrose.

'Oh, yes,' Grandpa said. 'A horribly polite young man. Let him fend off the Press.'

The phone rang again. 'Oh, hello, Cory,' George Rendell said, rolling his eyes at Emilie.

She started and shook her head violently.

Her grandfather smiled at her with rueful understanding. 'No,' he said into the phone. 'She isn't here at the moment. No, I've no idea when she'll be back. Yes, I'll tell her you called.'

When he had rung off Grandpa said drily, 'He sounded half crazy. Just as well you didn't answer the phone. No doubt he'll be round here soon. You had better not answer the door, either.'

The phone rang again.

'Good God!' Grandpa exclaimed, going red. 'How much longer is this going on?' This time it was one of his own friends, buzzing with curiosity. Grandpa cheered up a little talking to this man. 'Thank you, I'll give her your congratulations. Yes, a very big fish. She's going to have two big homes to run in future, but I'm sure she'll cope. Oh, I'm delighted.'

He had no sooner put the phone down when it rang again; another journalist wanted to talk to Emilie. Grandpa politely told the man to try Ambrose's public relations department. After that call he decided to switch the telephone on to the automatic answering machine.

Half an hour later, Aunt Rosa and Sophie arrived, Aunt Rosa exclaiming as soon as Grandpa opened the front door, 'Congratulations... Wonderful news... Wedding of the year... Clever girl... What a coup! He's so rich it's positively disgusting—she'll be in the lap of luxury for the rest of her life. Has he bought a ring yet?'

'Yes. Come in, Rosa,' George Rendell glumly told her.

Emilie was tense as she faced them both. Aunt Rosa kissed her, and demanded, 'Have you got a ring?'

Sophie stood watching; she was glittering and terrible, her eyes as black as night and her smile like a knife.

Emilie held out her hand. She was not yet used to wearing her ring; it felt heavy on her. Aunt Rosa stared, drawing a breath. 'My dear girl! It's magnificent.'

'It's a sapphire,' Emilie said, very conscious of Sophie's fixed stare focused on the ring, the whiteness of her face.

'A cushion-shaped sapphire,' Sophie said curtly. 'And from the look of it I'd say it is at least thirty carats, in a circular-cut diamond cluster on a platinum hoop, worth at a conservative estimate somewhere around a hundred thousand pounds.'

Aunt Rosa laughed. 'Very impressive, darling, but is it really worth that much? How close is she, Emilie?'

Amazed, Emilie said, 'Very close—you really know what you're talking about, don't you, Sophie? You're very clever.'

'You're cleverer,' Sophie bit out.

Her tone made Emilie even more nervous. 'It's beautiful, isn't it?' she quickly said, hoping to deflect any attack Sophie might be planning to make. 'Ambrose spent a long time choosing it. We sat in a jeweller's office and looked at dozens of rings—well, it seemed like dozens to me. I liked them all, but Ambrose kept saying no, until they produced this ring, and then he said, "That's it, that's the one!" I must admit, I was horrified when I heard the price, but Ambrose didn't turn a hair.'

'Why should he? He can afford it.'

George Rendell had a worried look. 'Drink, Rosa?' he asked, trying to change the subject. 'Sophie? What can I get you?'

'Too early for me,' she said. 'I'd rather just have coffee.'

'I'll make some,' Emilie hurriedly said, leaving the room, but Sophie followed her out to the kitchen.

She sat down and watched Emilie moving around, getting cups and saucers, a sugar-bowl, a cream-jug.

Casually, Sophie drawled, 'You must tell me your secret, darling. How did you get Ambrose to propose? Maybe my mistake was going to bed with him without holding out for a ring? Men never value what they get easily.'

Emilie drew breath, paling. Sophie watched her like a cat circling a mouse, waiting for the moment when it would pounce for the kill.

'You did know we were lovers, didn't you?'

Jealousy was a physical pain, a jagged stab of agony in Emilie's chest. She swallowed, and somehow said thinly, 'We don't talk about the past!'

Sophie smilingly watched her as if eager to see her bleed. 'Oh, you should! His past is crowded with incident—he's very good in bed, by the way. Or have you already found that out?'

'That's not something I'm going to discuss with you!'

Emilie faced Sophie, her chin lifted and her blue eyes level and defiant, and Sophie considered her, an ugly curl to her mouth.

'I suppose he's playing it by the book with you, you're so obviously a little virgin. Going to make him wait till the wedding-night, are you, darling?'

Emilie hated the sneer with which she said that.

Sophie laughed. 'I hope he isn't going to be disappointed. Ambrose can be ruthless.' She paused and an odd look came into her face. Her tone changed, and she said rapidly, 'Well, good luck, darling—you're going to need it, as you'll soon find out. Life is full of surprises.'

What did that mean? wondered Emilie, a little shiver running down her spine at something in Sophie's voice, in her eyes.

Sophie looked at her watch in a very obvious way. 'Oh, good heavens! Look at the time! Sorry, I'll have to skip the coffee. I have something urgent to do.'

She vanished in a hurry and Emilie slowly finished loading her tray, frowning. Why had Sophie suddenly run off like that? Emilie had a sinking feeling that she was up to something—but what?

George Rendell came into the kitchen and looked sharply at her. 'Sophie has left—did she upset you, Emilie?'

'She tried to.' Emilie gave him a wry smile.

George Rendell swore under his breath. 'Damned little cat! I knew she'd run her claws into you when she heard. Of course, she's jealous—take no notice of her.'

'I won't,' Emilie said, but that was easier said than done. She couldn't get out of her mind the images Sophie had deliberately conjured up. Ambrose had been her lover. There had been a sensual memory in her eyes, in the full redness of her mouth. It made Emilie sick to think of them together. How many other women had there been in his life? He hadn't told her; she hadn't liked to ask, but she didn't believe Sophie had been the only one.

She was out with Ambrose that evening, and went to bed late. She woke up at seven-thirty as usual, but when she went downstairs in her nightie and towelling robe she found the house empty. There was a note from her grandfather telling her that he had had a call from the mill to say there had been an accident there; he had had to go at once, but he would ring to let her know what had happened.

Emilie made herself some coffee and sat in the kitchen, sipping orange juice, gazing blankly out of the window. It was raining heavily. She was sick of winter weather— how soon would it be spring? She and Ambrose had agreed on a date for the wedding—he wanted it at the end of March. She had begun thinking about a wedding-dress; her mind drifted into daydreams about a Victorian-style crinoline, a long lace veil.

The doorbell rang; still daydreaming she went to answer it and saw Sholto with a sinking heart.

'I'm very busy, Sholto, you can't come in!' She was sorry for him, but uneasy too. Sholto was older than she was, but emotionally he was still a teenager, blind to other people's needs and feelings, only seeing what he wanted to see, only caring about himself.

'You can't marry him!' he burst out, his lower lip stuck out like a baby's. 'My God, Em, he's nearly forty, and you're half his age; you can't be in love with him, I don't believe it. It's his money, isn't it? That's what you're after?'

She was angry then, flushing indignantly. 'What a disgusting thing to say! Do you realise how insulting that is? Oh, go away, Sholto.'

She tried to shut the door, but he pushed on it, using his strong young shoulder to muscle the door open again.

'Don't. I'm sorry, Em! I didn't mean to insult you, I was just so angry and upset. I love you—it drives me crazy to think of you marrying anyone else!'

'You don't love me, Sholto! If you did, you'd want me to be happy.'

'That's just the point! How could you possibly be happy with Ambrose? He's too old for you.' Sholto threw his arms round her.

She struggled angrily. 'Let me go, Sholto!'

'No, listen . . . Darling Em, please listen . . .'

She shook her head, pushing at his chest. 'I'm not listening to anything until you let go of me!'

'I read an article in a magazine the other day,' he gabbled, overriding her. 'It said that girls who've never had any love from their dads fall for older men because they're looking for their father. Well, can't you see how that fits?'

Briefly, she looked startled, then crossly said, 'Don't give me any of that pyscho-babble, Sholto! I don't see Ambrose as a father-figure!'

'That's the point—you wouldn't see it, you're too close. It's like dreams; people never can work out their own dreams, however obvious they may be to other people. Em, think about it. Your father was always too busy to have time for you, you felt he didn't care about you. When you met Ambrose you confused the two of them; Ambrose is busy and powerful, like your dad, but he showed an interest in you. You're sleepwalking into this marriage, because you're all screwed up about your dad, but one day you'll wake up and realise what a terrible mistake you've made, and then you'll get badly hurt.'

'I love him, Sholto,' she insisted, and he groaned.

'Oh, Em...'

He was wearing a thin anorak, his collar turned up, rain dripping from his hair down his pale face. He looked like a sad little boy, and she couldn't help feeling sorry for him.

He saw her face change and pleaded, 'I'm so miserable, Em. I'm not sleeping or eating, you're making me ill.'

The trouble was, she believed him. He had no colour at all, and his eyes were underlined with shadows. She bit her lip, looking at him with compunction and troubled impatience.

'Why are you so stupid?' She looked him over. 'Your trainers are sodden! Take them off—Grandpa will kill me if he finds wet footprints on the carpets.'

He took off his trainers and anorak, and Emilie took them into the kitchen to dry them in front of the Aga. Sholto followed and sat by the range, hunched over the heat, looking very young and thin in his old jeans and dark blue sweatshirt.

'I'm so cold...' He shivered.

'What do you expect, going about in the pouring rain? You need your head examined.' She tossed him a towel. 'Dry your hair, you look half drowned.'

She poured him a cup of coffee and sat down at the table to drink her own, which was still warm.

'I've got another job,' Sholto told her. 'I'm going into a stockbrokers' office in the City of London. A friend of the family offered me a place.'

'Aren't you lucky?' That was part of his problem— he got things too easily, there was always someone to get him what he wanted. 'So you're leaving the bank?'

'I've left. I wasn't going on working for him once I knew he'd stolen you from me.'

'Sholto, he didn't steal me! I never belonged to you— how could he steal me?'

He looked sullen. 'He knew I loved you, but he took you away from me. That's how he operates in business. He's ruthless, he goes after whatever he wants without caring what happens to anyone who gets in his way. Well, he isn't getting away with it this time. I'm getting my own back.'

There was defiance in his voice, in his face. Emilie looked at him sharply, her instincts prickling. What was he planning?

'Sholto, don't do anything you'll regret!'

'I won't regret it!' he muttered.

She felt apprehension; Sholto had done something, something stupid, her intuition told her so. But what?

'What have you done, Sholto?' she asked him, and he shrugged, looking away.

'Seen today's papers?'

'No, why?' She got to her feet to find them, and as she did the doorbell rang. Sholto jumped up, spilling coffee.

'Don't answer it!'

The ringing went on; somebody had their thumb on the bell. Emilie couldn't stand the noise; she went into the hall and Sholto followed, grabbing his trainers and anorak.

'Em, listen... Don't...'

She took no notice of him. She opened the door and Ambrose came through it, slamming it behind him.

Emilie looked at him in shock—his face was dark, hard, violent with rage.

'Why? Why did you do it?' he burst out in a raw voice.

'What are you talking about?' Emilie turned pale, her blue eyes wide and alarmed.

'As if you didn't know!'

He hurled a folded newspaper at her; it fell to the floor.

'Read it!' Ambrose snarled.

Hands shaky, she picked it up, unfolded it and saw the front page. Across the top half of it was a large picture of herself and Ambrose; the official one his PR people had been giving out.

Then she read the headline and jerked as if she had had an electric shock.

'MEXICAN SLUM KID ON TOP'.

She drew in a horrified breath and Ambrose turned to give her a bitter look.

'Read it all. They really did some digging once they knew where to look!'

She went on staring at him nervously; he was so big and powerful in the black cashmere overcoat, his hands sheathed in black leather gloves, his face as hard as if it had been carved out of stone.

'Read it!' he ordered again through his teeth, and she hurriedly looked back at the newsprint.

They hadn't really got much detail—only the fact that Ambrose had been born in Mexico, the date and place of his birth, the names of his parents, their poverty, how many other children they had had, the dates of their deaths and the date when Ambrose first got a British passport and came to London. The pictures were more telling—a grey photograph of a huddle of shacks near Mexico City, one of ragged, barefoot children, a third of the beautiful house in Regent's Park where Ambrose now lived.

She looked up slowly. 'Oh, Ambrose... how did they find out?'

His face was harsh. 'Didn't you think Sholto would give it to the Press? Well, now we both know how it feels to be betrayed, don't we?'

'Sholto?' She was bewildered. 'What makes you think...?'

'I know you told Sholto everything I told you, so don't bother to try and lie your way out of it. I've been on to the journalist—he told me he got the whole story from Sholto.'

CHAPTER EIGHT

'SHOLTO?' She turned to look towards him, and it was at that instant that Ambrose realised Sholto was there.

He flashed a look across the hall, saw Sholto sitting on the bottom of the stairs, head bent, hurriedly tying the laces of his trainers with hands that shook.

Ambrose stiffened, his muscled body so tense that she saw a blue vein stand out in his neck. His eyes went from Sholto back to her, in her nightdress and robe.

'So it's true,' he said in a hoarse whisper. 'He's been here all night.'

She was appalled. 'Of course he hasn't, Ambrose! How can you...?'

'He's getting dressed!'

'No! You don't understand... His trainers were wet through, so I made him take them off and I put them on the radiator to dry.'

'Don't lie to me!' he snarled, his face harsh with cruelty. 'Do you think I'm stupid? He's obviously just got out of bed—and so have you!'

She was trembling, terrified at the look in his face. 'Sholto! Tell him the truth!' she appealed as Sholto stood up, shouldering into his anorak.

'The truth? Are you sure that's what you want me to tell him?' Sholto asked her insolently, and she was stricken.

'Sholto, for God's sake!'

'Sorry, Emilie, but I warned you,' he shrugged.

157

'Warned me about what?' she asked, bewildered by everything that was happening. 'Was it you who gave that story to the newspaper?'

His only answer was a grin. Ambrose slowly stripped off his leather gloves, pushed them into the pocket of his overcoat, took it off and threw it on a chair.

She gave Sholto a desperate look. 'Why are you doing this? Sholto, you know I didn't tell you anything about Ambrose... Who did? Tell him who told you. Tell him it wasn't me.'

'It wasn't her who told me,' Sholto drawled in Ambrose's direction, but his smile was mocking, contradicting what he said.

'Don't smirk at me, you little bastard!' Ambrose hit him so hard that Sholto fell back on the newel-post of the stairs. A gash opened on the side of his head.

Sholto grabbed one of George Rendell's walking-sticks from the umbrella-stand beside the front door. 'Touch me again and I'll smash your head in!' he threatened, blood trickling down the side of his face.

Ambrose reached for him, wrenched the stick from him and hurled it away. Sholto went into panic and bolted for the street with Ambrose hot on his heels.

'Let him go, Ambrose!' Emilie begged, trying to hold him back, but his powerful body was surging with such rage that she was dragged along with him, her heels digging into the carpet. She managed to slow him down, if not to stop him. Sholto got out of the house before Ambrose could catch up with him. He tore down the garden path and into his car.

Ambrose stopped in the open doorway and watched Sholto start the car and drive away through the pouring rain, a cloud of steam coming from the exhaust pipe. Only when he was out of sight did Ambrose slam the door shut again and turn his dark, glittering eyes on Emilie.

'You treacherous, unfaithful little tramp!'

She was really frightened now. She let go of him, backing away. 'Ambrose, I haven't done anything... I didn't tell Sholto about your childhood, I swear I didn't. I don't know how he found out—I haven't told anyone a word of what you told me. Not even Grandpa.'

His face had bitter distaste in it as he watched her. 'For the love of God, stop lying! It makes me sick. Your lover at least had the decency to admit what he'd done!'

She was getting more and more scared, but she tried to sound calm. 'He isn't my lover! How can you think——?'

'I believe what my eyes tell me,' he said in that harsh, cruel voice. 'You had a guilty look the minute you saw me, and I have never told anyone else in the word what I told you about my childhood, so how could Sholto have heard about it, except from you? You told him in bed, did you? While he was doing it to you?'

'No, Ambrose!' she said, feeling sick.

'How many times has he had you?'

She shuddered in dismay at his expression, his tone. 'Ambrose, don't! I swear to you—I've never been to bed with him.'

'Is he good? Better than me? He's younger, maybe he can keep it up longer. I can't say I wasn't warned—he told me that sooner or later you'd go back to him.'

She tried to put her arms round his neck, looking warily into his bitter, dangerous face.

'Ambrose, please, stop it. I love you. I've never been to bed with anyone else.'

He looked down at her and his eyes began to burn. She heard him breathing fast, thickly.

'My God, every time I look at you I can't believe it's possible. That lovely face, those clear blue eyes, they look so innocent. How could that face belong to a lying little cheat? I don't want to believe it, that's the irony of it. I want to believe in you—that's what you've done to me. I'm your accomplice. I've cheated myself, because I desperately wanted to find someone like you. Maybe it was my Mexican childhood... All my people have to comfort themselves with, for their terrible poverty and their lack of hope, is their images of the Madonna. You see the shrines at every street-corner, in every village, on the roads as you drive past. That's what I took you for! A pure, sweet, loving Madonna! How could I have been such a fool? Was I even the first? That night we first slept together... You convinced me you were a virgin but now I wonder—was that a charade too? Have you been sleeping with young Cory all the time?'

'No, Ambrose! Why won't you believe me? I didn't tell Sholto about your childhood and I've never slept with him. You must believe me!' He was terrifying her, he was talking so strangely. Her voice shook. 'I love you, I would never do anything to hurt you!'

He ran his thumb along the trembling curve of her mouth. 'I can't bear to think of him touching you.'

'I wouldn't let him!'

'Your mouth drives me crazy...' He groaned, staring at it, bent his head and began kissing her fiercely, with such insistence that her lips were forced back on her teeth, but she didn't dare try to stop him.

She held on to his neck, her body swaying closer, pressing into his from shoulder to thigh, her mouth given up to him without resistance. She must placate him, coax him, seduce him out of this angry mood.

He pushed her dressing-gown open, slid his hand inside her nightdress. As it touched her breast her nipples hardened, her body began to throb. Her senses were so heightened by the adrenalin of fear that at one touch desire ran hotly through her.

He slid his mouth down her neck and bit her; she moaned, her head hanging back.

Ambrose pulled her nightdress upwards, leaving her body naked to her breasts; his head went down, his mouth hotly sucking at her nipples, his hands moving lower, between her parted thighs.

Eyes closed, she trembled, moaning hoarsely.

'You see? Even now, I still want you,' he muttered. 'And you aren't stopping me—you want it too. You've been at it all night with that boy, but you're still ready to do it with me now, aren't you? Shall we do it here, on the floor?'

He pushed her backwards, downwards, her body tumbling helplessly to the floor, and fell on top of her, his knee forcing hers apart.

Emilie's eyes were open again, her face white, all the heat and sensuality suddenly gone.

'Ambrose, you're frightening me!'

He framed her face with his hands, staring from her mouth to her eyes. 'Do you know about the people who lived in Mexico before the Spaniards invaded the place? They were called Aztecs; they worshipped the sun, offered sacrifices to it—ripped out the hearts of living people. That's what you've done to me, ripped the heart out of me. How am I supposed to live without a heart?'

Emilie was increasingly frightened by the way he was talking. 'Please let me get up, Ambrose—you're hurting me... Let me go, please!'

'Let you go?' he repeated, his mouth twisting. 'To him? No, Emilie, I won't let you go. I'd rather kill you than let you go to another man.'

His hands came so swiftly she didn't even see them move until they were fastened around her throat, his hard thumbs pressing downwards, choking her.

Emilie gasped, tried to cry out, but couldn't. He was squeezing too strongly. She could scarcely breathe, her eyes had darkened, she dragged air into her lungs in terror, shaking like a leaf as it dawned on her.

He was going to kill her.

Her eyeballs seemed to be on fire, she was gasping and fighting for breath, clawing at the hands which gripped her throat, not even able to scream or plead with him.

'Oh, God!' Ambrose suddenly let go, the darkness in his stare clearing, shock in his white face. He stood up, pulled her to her feet, holding her shoulders as she swayed, coughing, one hand at her sore and bruised throat.

She was shaking, crying, too weak to stand; she sank down on to the bottom stair, covering her face with her hands, sobbing, too shocked to think about what had just happened.

'I'm sorry, Emilie,' she heard him mutter. 'God, I'm sorry. I went crazy—all I knew was I wanted to kill you, and I nearly did. I only just stopped myself in time. I don't know what to say...'

Reason had taken over, thank God. He had obeyed the long-embedded instincts born of hundreds of years of social conditioning, backed up by the commandment, Thou shalt not kill. It didn't mean he forgave her, or still loved her.

Her throat was bruised and swollen. It hurt to swallow.

Emilie ran the back of her hand over her wet eyes. She was thinking now, realising with a sick pang what she had to do. She looked down at her hand, at the dark blue flash of the sapphire, the glitter of the diamonds. Slowly, she took off her engagement-ring and held it out to him.

He didn't take it; he stared at it blankly, his face bleak, white.

'Take it,' she said, tears still trickling from under her lids.

He fished a clean handkerchief out of his pocket and put it in her hand.

'Dry your eyes.'

It could have been funny, that quiet paternal tone, in the circumstances—if it hadn't been so hurtful.

Silently she took the handkerchief, wiped her eyes, blew her nose, so miserable that it helped to have something practical to do.

Every time she swallowed, it hurt. It hurt even more to try to talk, but she forced herself, getting the words out in a hoarse whisper.

'I can't marry someone who doesn't believe a word I say. You must take your ring back.'

'What would I do with it? Keep it—give it to a charity, do what you like with it.' He turned away, picked up his overcoat, put it on. 'Goodbye, Emilie.'

As he opened the front door she cried out desperately, 'I didn't tell anyone about Mexico! And I have never slept with Sholto!' It might be the last chance she had to tell him so.

Ambrose looked back at her, his face stony, unrelenting. Emilie felt hopeless, but she tried one more time. 'I have never lied to you!'

For a second his face seemed confused, uncertain, and at that instant there was a flash of light from outside.

Ambrose jerked his head round, swore under his breath. 'Damn them to hell!'

'What is it?' Emilie cried out as the flash of light happened again.

Ambrose slammed the door shut. Outside she heard loud voices calling his name, calling hers.

Someone rattled the letterbox; eyes peered into the hall.

Ambrose got her shoulders and pushed her back into the kitchen. 'Is there a back exit?'

'Only through the garage. What's happening out there? Who are those people?'

'Your friends the Press,' he said bitterly. 'They're never satisfied. You've aroused their interest now, and you're going to have to suffer the consequences. They won't go away until they get another story, and then tomorrow they'll want some more. They're hyenas, living off dead men's bones.'

They were banging on the door and ringing the bell, shouting. Emilie was terrified.

'It sounds like a mob of them! How many are out there?'

'I didn't stop to count them, but there were at least a dozen.' Ambrose was pacing the floor, head bent, frowning blackly. 'How the hell am I going to get out of here? Where's your grandfather?'

'He had to go to the mill, there's been some sort of accident.'

'Has he taken his car?'

'Yes, of course.' Emilie watched him, her heart aching. 'Ambrose, I never told anyone anything, not even

Grandpa.' Then she thought of something, biting her lip. 'The only time I came close to it was...'

'Was when?'

'Well, I've been reading books on Mexico...' A little colour came into her face and she gave him a shy look through her lashes. 'I wanted to find out about the place you came from. I had some in here, while I was cooking Christmas lunch, and Sophie...'

'Ah,' he said on an indrawn breath. 'Sophie?'

'She noticed them and asked me why I was so interested in Mexico—but I didn't tell her, Ambrose! I've never repeated what you told me to a living soul.'

He was frowning, walking to and fro, his face implacable. Suddenly he halted. 'I have a lot to do, I can't stay here. I'll have to run the gauntlet of those bastards out there. Come to the door with me, and as soon as I'm through it put your whole weight on it and slam it shut to keep them out or they'll be all over the house in two seconds. Then go upstairs, get dressed, and stay there. Don't answer the phone or go to the door. Ring your grandfather and tell him what's going on, warn him to stay away all day.'

'He can't stay there forever!'

'No, but I expect most of the Press will follow me. I'll have some men round here as soon as I can arrange it, to keep the rest of the pack at bay long enough for your grandfather to have a chance to get indoors, and then they'll stand guard at the front door to stop them constantly ringing the bell and knocking.'

He walked out of the kitchen and she followed. At the front door he took a deep breath.

'Ready?'

She nodded. 'Ambrose, please...'

He ignored her. The door opened and she saw the circle of faces, the flashing of cameras, heard a muddle of voices.

'Ambrose, is it true...?'

'What does it feel like to come from working on a city dump to running a London bank?'

'Ambrose, let's have a smile...'

'Hey, Ambrose, can we see the girl?'

'How did you get into the country, Ambrose? Are you an illegal immigrant?'

'Ambrose, bring the girl out here for us...'

Under his breath Ambrose muttered fiercely, 'Now!'

She slammed the door and leaned on it, shaking, tears running down her face.

Outside she heard the shouting continue.

'If you want a statement, come to my office at eleven o'clock this morning,' Ambrose said.

'Is the girl going to be there?'

'Did she know about your background?'

'What do her family think about all this?'

He didn't answer any of their questions. She heard shuffling, pushing—they were moving further away—then there was the sound of a car starting, and the pack of reporters and cameramen surged after it.

He had gone. It was over. She couldn't believe it. Love had come out of nowhere like a hot desert wind, blowing her life into new patterns; now it had blown away and she was left desolate.

She swallowed her tears, the movement of her throat agonising. She almost wished he had killed her. She wouldn't be in this pain now if he had.

How could he believe such terrible things? If he loved her, why would he think her capable of lying, cheating, betraying him? He didn't know her or he wouldn't believe it. He had never known her. And if he hadn't known her, how could he ever have loved her?

That hot desert wind had simply conjured up a mirage of love. Now it had dissolved back into the desert, leaving her life empty.

Sobbing, she crawled up the stairs to her room, her body heavy as lead, trembling. She felt unclean. The avid curiosity of the men outside had been like being undressed in public. She took a long shower, scrubbed herself unmercifully, then slowly got dressed in the grey winter light. Rain fell persistently outside, trickled down the windows like tears, ran in the gutters, soaked into the ground. The sound of traffic was hushed by it; she couldn't even hear the running of the river beyond the busy Embankment.

She tentatively peered through the curtains at the street. It seemed empty; for a second she thought the Press had left, then she noticed someone in a car lighting a cigarette and realised that there were half a dozen parked cars out there, and all of them held men watching the house.

Emilie fell back. She went to the telephone then and rang the mill. She was put through to her grandfather, who sounded disturbed, grave.

'Emilie, have you seen today's newspapers?'

'That's why I'm ringing,' she said huskily, trying not to break down—it would only upset Grandpa. 'The Press are camped out on the doorstep. Ambrose says you should stay at the mill all day.'

'Is he there?'

'No, he has been here, but he has gone to the bank. He's holding a Press conference this morning.'

'So you're alone there? I'm coming home.'

'No, Grandpa. Ambrose is arranging for some body-guards to come and stand guard on the house, keep the Press away. Don't come home yet or you'll have a problem getting into the house. It would be best to do as Ambrose said.'

Her grandfather was silent for a moment, then he said, 'Did you know about all this Mexican stuff, Emilie?'

'Yes,' she whispered. 'But I don't know who told the Press—I hadn't breathed a word about it, so how did the Press get hold of the story? Ambrose says it was Sholto who told them, but I didn't tell Sholto.'

'Are you all right? You sound very upset—what the hell is going on, Emilie? I think I should come home at once. I don't like the idea of you being alone there.'

'No, please, I'll be OK,' she urgently said, and he sighed.

'I must say, I can't help admiring Ambrose—when you know where he came from, I mean. He must have had a lot of courage and determination to get to where he is now. I'm impressed. This has entirely changed the way I see him.'

'Yes,' she said, smiling.

'So he's half Mexican—explains his colouring. I always thought he must be Mediterranean.'

She couldn't bear talking about Ambrose any more. 'You didn't tell me,' she interrupted. 'The accident...was it serious? What happened?'

'One of the apprentices got a hand trapped in a roller last night; I'm afraid he may lose it, but the hospital are doing their best. Stupid boy, disobeyed all the safety rules.' Emilie listened as George Rendell talked on about the accident at the mill. Then he paused. 'Well, I'll see you later, then, Emilie, but if you need me, ring me at once.'

Later that morning, Emilie saw most of the Press cars drive away, leaving only one parked outside, with a cameraman in it. She went downstairs at noon to make herself a piece of toast, with a boiled egg, for lunch, turned on the recorded messages and listened to the stream of calls from journalists on women's magazines and newspapers, radio and television.

Among them was a call from Sholto, pleading, 'Em, please talk to me. I'm at home. I just want to make sure you're OK. I'm worried about you, please ring me.'

She rang him at once. 'Sholto?'

He recognised her voice. 'Oh, Em... Are you OK?'

'As if you care! How could you tell such lies about me?'

'I was getting my own back on him, and he deserved it. I'm sorry if I landed you in it, though. I don't want to hurt you, Em. That's why I've rung, to make sure you're OK. I love you, you know that. After I'd driven off I started to worry. I was afraid he might turn nasty. I shouldn't have left you alone with him.'

'You shouldn't have lied to him! You made him very angry with me!'

She heard Sholto's intake of breath. 'What did he do to you? Are you hurt? What...?'

'No, I'm not hurt—no thanks to you! If you really do care about me, you'll tell me the truth. I didn't tell you about Mexico, and you know it—so how did you find out? If you don't tell me, I'll never speak to you again, and I mean that, Sholto!'

'That's blackmail.' His voice was outraged, childishly incredulous. Sholto might stoop to lies and blackmail, but he didn't expect her to.

'I mean it, so tell me the truth—who told you about Mexico?'

There was a silence, then, 'Sophie,' he sullenly admitted.

Emilie had known all along—it had to have been Sophie who had somehow picked up on her nervousness, her reluctance to talk about Mexico. Sophie had antennae like radar.

'How did she find out the details? Ambrose swore he'd never told anyone else about it.'

'She said she picked up a clue from you, and told that guy Wheeler when she suspected.'

'Wheeler?' For a second Emilie was blank, then she made the connection. 'Gavin Wheeler?'

'That's right. He hates Kerr too; he thinks he ought to get more of the profits from the deals he puts together for the bank. He doesn't see why Ambrose Kerr should get the lion's share. He's jealous of him. Sophie saw you reading books on Mexico and was curious when you went pink and kept trying to change the subject. She said you looked so agitated it had to be important.'

Emilie closed her eyes, groaning. 'So it is all my fault!'

'Sophie's street-smart, and you aren't,' Sholto said ruefully. 'Anyway, Sophie told Wheeler she suspected Ambrose had some Mexican connection, so Wheeler flew over there and did some digging. He found out that Kerr has dual nationality—a British passport and a Mexican one. Wheeler came up with a lot of official stuff—a birth certificate, death certificates of his parents, photos of the slums where he was born. He even dug up people who remembered him, and he tracked down his sisters. But they wouldn't talk to Wheeler. He managed to hire a photographer to snatch some pictures, though. Sophie gave the whole package to me and told me which newspaper to give it to. She told me they would pay me a lot of money for an exclusive on Ambrose, and they did.

Rags to riches makes a good headline. They paid me well.' Sholto sounded defiant again. 'Well, I had a good job at the bank until he made it impossible for me to stay there. I could do with the money.'

Angrily, Emilie said, 'I don't want to see you again—stay out of my way in future. Don't ring me, and don't come here.'

'Em!' he cried in protest, but she put the phone down, feeling chilled, depressed. Sholto's jealousy, Sophie's envy, had ruined her life.

If she could only get Sholto to confess he had lied, admit who had really told him, Ambrose might...

She sighed heavily.

Sholto wasn't going to do that. He had achieved his aim—he had split her from Ambrose, wrecked their relationship, and hurt Ambrose by doing so. Why would he undo all that by telling the truth?

She put her ring away in a drawer. Her hand felt naked without it. She would have to tell Grandpa when he got home tonight. He hadn't approved of their engagement. It was ironic that the revelations about Ambrose's past had made Grandpa like him more. When she told him the engagement was off he would be sorry for her, and the thought of his pity made her wince. She wished she lived alone on a desert island where she needn't worry about other people. Coping with the pain of her broken engagement was hard enough without having to dread other people's reactions.

Downstairs the doorbell rang again, and she ignored it until she heard the baying of the hounds outside—shouted questions, flashbulbs exploding.

Was it Grandpa?

She ran to the window to look out and saw grey hair in the centre of a press of reporters, all pushing and shoving.

Emilie tore down the stairs and pulled the door open, shouting, 'Let him alone! Let him go!' She grabbed the old man and began tugging him into the house. The photographers all turned their cameras on to her, so she kept her head down as she backed inside, ignoring the questions being yelled at her.

'Who is it, Emilie?'

'Is it your grandfather, Emilie?'

'Can we just have one of you two together?'

'Did you know Ambrose was born in a cardboard box?'

'Is it true he got rich through the Mexican Mafia?'

'How did he make his money, Emilie?'

She and her rescued captive finally made it through the front door, but the Press tried to come in with them.

'Get out or I'll call the police!' Emilie threatened, pushing on the door. The heaving mob resisted; several had planted their feet in the door to stop her shutting it.

Suddenly from behind them came a sound of running and several very large, brawny men leapt on the journalists and began hurling them to one side bodily.

Startled, the Press fell back and one of the newcomers told Emilie, 'Get that door shut now, miss! We've been sent by Mr Kerr. Don't worry, we'll keep them away from the house from now on!'

Emilie thankfully closed the door and leaned on it, breathing fast, tears in her eyes.

'Oh, Grandpa! Why on earth did you come back? It must have been so frightening for you! Ambrose told you to stay away until later...'

Her voice died away as she looked into the man's face and saw with shock that it wasn't her grandfather. It was Ewan Wingate, her grandfather's old enemy.

CHAPTER NINE

'WHAT are you doing here?' she gasped.

'I wanted to see either your grandfather or Ambrose,' Ewan Wingate told her, breathing thickly. He wasn't quite as old as Grandpa, but he was in his late sixties, a stooped, grey-haired man with pale blue eyes, and the shock of his encounter with the Press had obviously disturbed him. He was pale and sweating. 'Can I sit down? I'm feeling a bit odd.'

'Yes, of course,' she said anxiously, and guided him into the sitting-room. 'Can I get you anything?'

'A glass of water, thank you,' he said, undoing his dark overcoat and taking it off.

She hung it up in the hall and got him a glass of water. When she got back, she found him leaning back in an armchair with his eyes shut. He opened them to take the water, and sipped it slowly. In the street they could hear the Press arguing with Ambrose's security men. Ewan Wingate glanced towards the window. 'How long have you had to put up with that?'

'Ever since early this morning. I'm afraid Ambrose is at the bank and Grandpa is at the mill, Mr Wingate.' She couldn't help the faint coldness in her tone—he had taken the mill away from them, after all.

He gave her a shrewd look. 'I'm sorry about the take-over, Emilie. When Ambrose suggested it to me I jumped at it.' He made a wry face. 'I've had a tussle going with your grandfather for so long that I've almost lost sight of the reason for it, or the fact that we were once close friends. I couldn't resist the chance to grab his firm from him. I thought it would be my big triumph—but once I'd done it, somehow it all fell flat for me. It seems crazy, but I miss the rivalry we've had all these years. George is my oldest friend, as well as my chief rival. Getting rid of him was like getting rid of part of myself. That's why I put Stephen in to manage the mill. I knew George liked him, and it would soften the blow, and that's why I agreed to Ambrose's suggestion that George stayed on as a consultant.'

'So it was him who suggested that?' she thought aloud.

Ewan Wingate nodded. 'And I jumped at the chance to... Oh, I don't know—re-establish the status quo, I suppose!'

Emilie softened; he was looking old and frail, like Grandpa. 'Is that why you're here? To try to make peace with him?'

He smiled at her, his colour rather better now and his breathing almost normal. 'Don't ever tell your grandfather this—but I'm really very fond of the old devil, and I feel bad about having taken over his firm. I have a lot of respect for Ambrose, too. When I read the papers this morning, I felt very sorry for him. He's such a private man, with a lot of dignity. He must hate having his name dragged through the papers and his past paraded for millions of strangers to read about! I just felt he might need some support from a friend. I came here because I thought he would be with you and George; I'd tried his home and been told he was out, and the bank is closed on Sundays.'

'To the public, yes, but Ambrose is giving a Press conference there this morning.'

'Then I'll go over there,' Ewan Wingate said, getting heavily to his feet, leaning on her as she hurriedly came

to help him. 'Thank you, my dear.' He put on his overcoat again. 'It sounds quiet out there now. Ambrose's
men have obviously got the situation under control. Will
you be all right here alone? Wouldn't you like to come
with me?'

'No, I'll be fine,' she said. 'But thank you, Mr
Wingate. You're very kind. I'll tell Grandpa you called.'

He grimaced. 'Tell him . . . I'm sorry . . .'

She nodded, smiling. 'I will.'

He put his shoulders back like a soldier facing battle.
'OK, then, open the door, my dear.'

She pulled the door open and Ewan Wingate went out.
At once two of the security men appeared and it was
under their escort that he made his way back to his
parked car. Emilie shut the door again, went to the phone
and rang her grandfather.

'I think it's safe for you to come home now. Ambrose
has security men outside, they'll keep the Press away
from you.'

'Are you OK, darling?' George Rendell asked
anxiously.

'I'm fine,' she lied, glad he couldn't see her face.

'Well, I'll be there as soon as I can.'

He arrived just over an hour later and had no problem
at all with the Press. There was only one car left outside
and the security men kept its occupants at bay while
George Rendell made it to the house.

Emilie told him about Ewan Wingate's visit, and
Grandpa looked his amazement.

'Well, that's . . . decent of him . . . You say he has gone
to the bank to see Ambrose? He is a generous man. I
have to grant him that, the old weasel.'

Emilie laughed. 'He called you an old devil!'

Grandpa seemed flattered. 'Oh, he did, did he? Well, he needn't think he's going to get round me with compliments.'

The phone began to ring again, and the answering machine cut in to take the call.

'That been going on all day?' Grandpa asked, and she wryly nodded.

'In fact, I'd better clear the tape again in a minute—most of them are calls from reporters. I just wipe the tape and start again.' She saw the light go out, which meant the current call had ended, so she switched on the playback to make sure none of the calls was important. As she expected, most of them were from the Press, but one was from Aunt Rosa, sounding agitated.

'Oh, George...I have to talk to you. Please, ring me as soon as you can, it's urgent.'

'I suppose she's read the Sunday papers too,' George Rendell drily said, as Emilie wiped the tape. 'But I'd better ring her or she'll come round here!'

He dialled Aunt Rosa's number. 'Hello? It's George, Rosa.'

He listened in silence, then his voice rose sharply. 'What? Slow down, Rosa... How do you know...? Ambrose? But how does he...?'

Emilie had stiffened; she watched him intently, her nerves jumping. She could hear Aunt Rosa's voice far off, a tinny little gabbling. What on earth was she saying?

'OK, Rosa, if that's what you want.' George Rendell rolled his eyes upwards in Emilie's direction, a silent comment on whatever Aunt Rosa was saying. 'Of course you can stay the night. Very well, take a taxi. We'll expect you.'

He put the phone down and turned to Emilie, his mouth tight with irritation.

'We just got landed with Rosa. I couldn't refuse, she's in such a state over Sophie, but it's going to be a bore having her here. I can't stand the woman.'

'What's happened to Sophie? You said something about Ambrose... What was that about?' Had Ambrose found out that Sophie had been the one who gave Sholto the details of his past and told him to take them to the Press?

'Sophie has run off with someone! I couldn't make head nor tail of what Rosa was telling me, she was so incoherent. Apparently she got up to find Sophie hadn't come home the night before. Rosa said it wasn't unusual for Sophie to go to an all-night party, she thought nothing of it at first, but Sophie usually rings to tell her when she will be home. No call came, and then Ambrose rang up, asking for Sophie. Rosa was so hysterical I couldn't make out what Ambrose had said, except that it has put the fear of God into Rosa.'

'It was Sophie who dug out all those details about Ambrose,' Emilie said huskily. 'That may be what this is all about. If Ambrose has discovered that...'

George Rendell stared at her, dumbfounded. 'Sophie is behind all this? My God...I wouldn't have thought even she would go so far. She must be mad. Ambrose will sack her, you can count on it.' He ran his hands through his thin grey hair, groaning. 'This is all too much for me. What a day! I've been up since six, because of that accident, and then all this!'

'Why don't you lie down for a while? You look terrible. I'll cope with Aunt Rosa.'

'I can't leave her to you!'

'Of course you can. She just wants to pour out her troubles—I don't mind listening to her.'

'Well, if you're sure...' He wanted to be talked into it; he was grey and weary. Emilie was worried by the look of him. He was too old for all this trauma.

He went up to bed and Emilie went into the kitchen to prepare a light snack for all three of them. She had only just begun making a salad when the doorbell went. Taking off her apron, Emilie went to the door. Aunt Rosa had got here half an hour earlier than expected. She opened the door, a polite smile ready. 'Hello, Aunt Rosa...'

Her words died in her throat as she saw Ambrose standing there, broad-shouldered and powerful in black jeans and a black leather jacket, his face dark and grim.

She fell back and let him in, and he closed the door behind him.

Emilie faced him uncertainly, bracing herself for whatever was to come, her head up, and, under her carefully applied make-up, her skin as pale as death.

His grey eyes searched her face; his brows met. 'You look terrible.'

'I don't feel wonderful,' she agreed with irony.

He pushed his hands into the belt of his jeans, leaning against the wall, his head bent and a lock of dark hair tumbling over his temples.

'All right; I deserve that. Emilie...I don't know what to say to you. I'm sorry doesn't begin to cover it. I realise how angry you are, how hurt—you have every right to be, too. I have no excuses. God knows I should have realised you wouldn't have done anything like that—but I was jealous of young Cory, and right from the beginning I've had an inferiority complex.'

'An inferiority complex?' she repeated, incredulous. 'You?'

Of all the men in the world Ambrose was the last you would associate with anything like that!

He gave her a grim, unsmiling glance then, pushing the thick lock of black hair out of his eyes.

'I couldn't forget I was years older than you!'

'I kept telling you it didn't bother me!'

'Not now, but how will you feel in ten years' time?'

'How do I know? You can't avoid risks, Ambrose! Life isn't like that.' She stopped dead. 'All this is academic now. It's over between us.'

He looked at her fixedly, his grey eyes glittering, glazed, as if with tears.

'I came to tell you how bitterly I regret blaming you for the newspaper story. I know now who really fed that stuff about me to Sholto. I got it out of him half an hour ago.'

She started. 'You've been to see him?'

He nodded. 'He told me everything. He said he'd already confessed to you.'

'Yes. He told me on the phone. He does have some good instincts, you know. He rang to make sure I was OK.'

Ambrose's mouth twisted furiously. 'A pity he lied in the first place!'

She gave him a wary, anxious look. 'How did you get him to talk?' What had he done to Sholto to get the truth out of him?

Ambrose's mouth indented with sardonic cynicism. 'Don't ask.'

She flinched. 'You didn't hit him?'

He didn't answer, and his grey eyes were level and unreadable as they stared back at her.

'Oh, poor Sholto!' she said, sorry for him in spite of everything. Sholto had a lot of faults, but he was weak

rather than wicked, and he was very scared of Ambrose.
He must have been petrified when Ambrose caught up
with him. 'I hope you didn't really hurt him?'

'It wasn't necessary. Once he knew I would hurt him
if I had to, he told me what I wanted to know. I had
already guessed most of it. Once you told me you suspected Sophie I tried to find her, and failed. She wasn't
at home, hadn't been there all night—her mother had
no idea where she was, and was on the point of ringing
the police. I had been trying to get in touch with Gavin
Wheeler too—he wasn't answering his phone so I sent
someone round to find him. A neighbour said Gavin
had driven off last night in a car loaded with luggage.'
Ambrose looked drily at her. 'Sophie was with him.'

Emilie's eyes were rounded. 'You mean they've gone
away together?'

Ambrose gave a cynical smile. 'They both believe in
mixing business with pleasure. Sophie has a very good
head on her shoulders, more like a man's than a
woman's; she is clever, ambitious, with an intuitive grasp
of the way money moves, what is going to happen in
the markets worldwide, which investments to buy or sell.
She will be valuable to Gavin on that side of things.
Gavin himself is shrewd, devious, cunning—a sort of
human corkscrew. All they needed was a lot of money
to stake them in a business venture.'

There was something odd in his tone. Emilie looked
sharply at him. 'Is there something you're not telling
me?'

'While I was at the bank a thought occurred to me.
I got some of the senior staff in to check through our
cash holdings.' He paused, looking at Emilie, his mouth
curling. 'Sophie and Gavin haven't just eloped, they went
off with a small fortune in bearer bonds.'

Blankly she asked, 'Bearer bonds? What are they?'

He smiled at her. 'Sorry. Well, basically, they're pieces of paper which promise to pay the bearer a sum of money. They have no name on them—whoever holds them can cash them, no questions asked, especially in certain third-world countries. Sophie knew we had some in a safe.'

'You mean...she's stolen them?'

He nodded. 'I've contacted the police, but they've had nearly twenty-four hours' start. They could be in South America by now, with half a million of the bank's money.'

Emilie drew a shaken, incredulous breath. 'That much?'

He smiled wryly. 'Sophie didn't take the risk for peanuts.'

'You seem very calm about this.' She would have expected him to be angrier, more bitter.

'I've been through so much trauma today that I think I've lost my capacity to be amazed,' Ambrose said. 'Although I didn't think Gavin was such a fool. Half a million won't last forever, not these days. Of course Gavin's clever; he worked directly to me, not actually for the bank. He isn't a banker, he's an asset assessor.'

'I've never been sure what that means.'

'He researches companies, uncovers their weaknesses and their strengths, works out the best way of attacking them. I've no doubt that that expertise is what he plans to offer to clients in the future, on his own behalf, instead of mine.'

'He envied you, you know. Sholto said...'

'Yes, he took great pleasure in telling me, too, how much Gavin resented and hated me.' Ambrose grimaced. 'It was Gavin who flew to Mexico to dig up everything he could about me, hoping to find something really discreditable.'

She gave him a nervous look from under lowered lashes. 'It was my fault Sophie picked up on that. I shouldn't have been so jumpy when she looked at the book I was reading. She can be very quick.'

'She was jealous of you—that sharpened her instincts. She and Gavin have a lot in common. He envied me my money and my power; she envied everything you had.'

She shivered, her skin deathly pale. 'It's horrible—knowing someone is jealous of you, is always watching you enviously. It makes your skin creep.'

'Don't look so sad, darling,' Ambrose said huskily, putting an arm round her.

For a second she almost turned her face into his warm, strong body, then she remembered, and stiffened, pushing him away.

'Don't!' she broke out in a choked, confused voice. One touch and she had been weakening. He had such a strong hold over her, in spite of the way he had hurt her. 'You'd better go!'

His hands fell to his sides. He stood there, looking at her, a nerve jumping beside his mouth, his eyes leaping with fire.

'Emilie... I know I don't deserve it—but won't you give me a second chance? I love you, you know I love you... if anything, too much. I would never have been so angry if I hadn't been so terrified of losing you.'

'I can't!' she cried out, on the point of tears. 'Don't you see? You don't trust me! I swore to you that I hadn't told Sholto about Mexico, but you didn't believe me.'

'I was in shock, Emilie! I've always been afraid people would find out the sort of background I came from, and when I saw all that in the papers it was one of my worst nightmares come true!'

'You wouldn't even believe me when I told you I hadn't let Sholto make love to me! You actually accused me of having slept with him all along... You said you weren't even sure now that I had been a virgin when I slept with you! If you really loved me, you wouldn't doubt me.'

'I didn't mean half I said, I was just talking wildly. I was crazy, Emilie! Out of my mind with jealousy and suspicion.'

She looked at him with anguish. 'How do I know it won't happen again? I couldn't stand it, Ambrose. You made me very unhappy, accusing me... refusing to believe me...'

'I know, Emilie,' he said on a deep sigh. 'I learnt in a hard school never to trust anyone. For so long I only had myself to rely on—it isn't easy to start trusting now.'

She was moved, thinking of his childhood, her hand involuntarily going to her throat.

She must have pushed aside the high-necked sweater hiding the bruises he had made. Ambrose suddenly winced, turning even whiter.

'My God...' He pulled the neck of the sweater down and stared at the bruises, groaning. 'I did those? Emilie... Sorry doesn't cover it, does it? You're right, you would be insane to have me anywhere near you after that.'

She looked at him through her lashes, aching with pain and desire. 'I ought to hate you,' she said huskily.

She felt his body tense. 'Do you?'

'So much it's like dying,' she whispered, and heard his sharp intake of breath.

'Emilie...'

'You might at least kiss them better,' she said, tilting her head back so that her whole throat was exposed.

Ambrose's arm encircled her waist, his other hand at the back of her head. His mouth softly, lingeringly, brushed across the bruises.

She felt the slow shudder of passion running through him. Swaying closer, her head came up and their mouths met with wild hunger. She ran her arms around his neck, clinging to him, aware of every inch of the strong male body touching her.

He broke off the kiss a few minutes later, breathing thickly, looked down at her, his eyes dark.

'Emilie, I love you—don't torment me. You won't send me away, after kissing me like that?'

She shook her head, her eyes cloudy with desire. 'I ought to—I must be crazy not to—but the trouble is, I love you. I can't bear to lose you.'

His arms closed convulsively around her, held her tightly, possessively. He groaned, closing his eyes, so pale he looked as if he might faint. 'Darling. I swear I'll believe every word you say in future, and I'll try not to be jealous of younger men.'

'I still don't know how on earth you could think that any woman would prefer Sholto Cory to you!'

He grimaced wryly. 'He's very good-looking.'

'He's sweet, and quite pretty,' she agreed. 'But he is a boy—not a man. He has a lot of growing up to do.'

'But he is your age, I'm not.'

'Sholto isn't my age! I'm far more adult than he is. The difference between me and Sholto is that I grew up in a tougher world. I had to nurse a dying mother; I had a father who didn't want to be bothered with me. Sholto has been spoilt and indulged all his life. We have very little in common, in fact.'

Ambrose was still, staring down at her intently, his face serious.

She smiled at him. 'And you and I have a lot in common, don't we? We both learnt to cope at an early age; we learnt to live without love; we learnt to be lonely and survive. The age-gap that bothers you so much doesn't bother me at all. You have so much I need, Ambrose. I think I can give you what you need, too. We both want a family life again; I want to have your baby, to make a home for us both. Passion isn't the only cement that bonds people—it will work out, Ambrose. Let's live our lives and be happy together without worrying about the future.'

He pulled her closer, put his head down on top of her hair, holding her. She leaned on him, her face burrowing into his body, hearing the strong, rhythmic beat of his heart under her cheek.

The silence was a promise, stronger than words. We will be happy, she thought, her eyes closed, surrounded by his warmth and love.

The jangle of the doorbell made them both jump. Ambrose groaned, lifting his head.

'Your grandfather?'

Emilie sighed. 'Aunt Rosa, I'm very much afraid—I was expecting her when you arrived. She's so upset about Sophie running off we had to tell her to come here. Grandpa is upstairs, resting. He looked very tired, so I sent him to bed.'

Ambrose looked aghast. 'She's going to be staying here?'

The doorbell jangled again.

'I'd better let her in!' Emilie said, moving towards the door. 'Before the Press nobble her.'

'They've mostly gone—my men are keeping the few who are left at a distance.'

Emilie opened the door, and Aunt Rosa tottered into the house on very high heels, moving on a cloud of musky French perfume.

'Oh, my dear... this is terrible. She didn't even say goodbye,' Aunt Rosa told Emilie, kissing her cheek. 'I still can't believe Sophie has done this to me.' She put a small lace handkerchief to her eyes and dabbed them, then she saw Ambrose and exclaimed eagerly, 'Oh, Ambrose! Have you heard any news yet? Have you found out anything?'

He shook his head. 'Only what I told you. She has definitely gone away with Gavin Wheeler.'

From the stairs George Rendell said, 'I'm sure Sophie will be in touch, Rosa, as soon as she's settled somewhere, then you can go and visit her.'

'But how could she do this to me?' wailed Aunt Rosa. 'She must know I'll be desperately worried.'

George Rendell came down and put an arm around her shoulders. 'Come and sit down, my dear, let me get you a brandy... You need something strong, for the shock.'

He led Rosa into the sitting-room. Ambrose looked down at Emilie, his mouth twisting. 'Not as bad a shock as she's going to get when it comes out that her daughter is being hunted by Interpol for embezzlement.'

'Poor Aunt Rosa. She'll die of shame.' Emilie had never actually been fond of her, but she couldn't help being sorry for her aunt now. She had been so proud of Sophie; this must be very hard on her.

'Nobody dies of shame,' Ambrose said drily. 'I used to think I might if it came out about my past. Until I met you I had such haunted dreams, my darling. I have tried all my life to shake off my past, but it wouldn't leave me alone. I was paranoid about it. When I saw those newspaper stories it was like my worst dream coming true. I thought my life here would be shattered—but I've been surprised by the way people reacted. I've had phone calls all day; people have come to the bank to see me—friends and colleagues have all been so kind.'

'Did Ewan Wingate find you?'

He nodded, smiling. 'He's a great old chap, isn't he? I was touched by him coming to see me, to promise me his support whatever happened.'

'He admires you,' she gently said, and Ambrose looked startled.

'Well, I don't know about that—but he seems to like me, and that I do value. What I hadn't realised was that they all knew very well that I didn't come from the same, safe background as themselves. I hadn't been to school with any of them, and they knew it. I hadn't got the right credentials from the start. My accent is a little too perfect, maybe—I learnt to talk in elocution lessons. I had a strong Mexican accent when I first arrived. And also these men all know each other, their families all know each other—it's a very small world they inhabit, and they all knew I was an outsider. I thought I was fooling them, but I never did. They just accepted me as a man who could make money. Oh, they wondered where I came from—but were too polite to ask. Now they know, and, if anything, they seem to admire me for having got to the top without any help or family back-up.'

Emilie nodded. 'The rags to riches story—it's everyone's favourite fairy-tale.' She framed his face with her hands. 'No more haunted dreams, darling. From now on, you must never forget that it doesn't matter where

you came from—all that counts is who you are, and you
are someone very special. I love you, Ambrose.'

He held her, his cheek against her hair, and laughed
huskily. 'In some ways this has been the worst day of
my life—a nightmare came true, someone embezzled a
fortune from the bank, and I almost lost you. But now
that I've got you back, I don't give a damn about the
rest of it. If I've got you, nothing else matters.'

Coming Next Month

HARLEQUIN PRESENTS®

THE BEST HAS JUST GOTTEN BETTER

#1833 THE FATHER OF HER CHILD Emma Darcy
Lauren didn't want to fall in love again—but when she saw Michael all her good resolutions went out the window. And when she learned he was out to break her heart she vowed never to see him again. But it was too late....

#1834 WILD HUNGER Charlotte Lamb
Book Four: *SINS*
Why was Gerard, famous foreign correspondent, following Keira? She could hardly believe he was interested in the story of a supermodel fighting a constant battle with food. No, he wanted something more....

#1835 THE TROPHY HUSBAND Lynne Graham
(9 to 5)
When Sara caught her fiancé being unfaithful, her boss, Alex, helped pick up the pieces of her life. But Sara wondered what price she would have to pay for his unprecedented kindness.

#1836 THE STRENGTH OF DESIRE Alison Fraser
(This Time, Forever)
The death of Hope's husband brought his brother, Guy, back into her life, and left her with two legacies. Both meant that neither Hope nor Guy would be able to forget their erstwhile short-lived affair.

#1837 FRANCESCA Sally Wentworth
(Ties of Passion, 2)
Francesca was used to having the best of everything—and that included men. The uncouth Sam was a far cry from her usual boyfriends, but he was the only man who had ever loved her for what she was rather than what she had.

#1838 TERMS OF POSSESSION Elizabeth Power
Nadine needed money—and Cameron needed a child. His offer was extraordinary—he would possess her body and soul and the resulting baby would be his. But the arrangements were becoming complicated...

HARLEQUIN PRESENTS®

**brings you the best books
by the best authors!**

EMMA DARCY
Award-winning author
"Pulls no punches..."   —*Romantic Times*

Watch for:
**#1833 The Father of Her Child
by Emma Darcy**

Lauren didn't want to fall in love again—but
when she saw Michael all her good resolutions
went out the window....

Harlequin Presents—the best has just gotten better!
Available in September wherever
Harlequin books are sold.

Look us up on-line at: http://www.romance.net

TAUTH-12

THE PAST
Guy had once been the only man
Hope could turn to.

THE PRESENT
Now he was back!

THE FUTURE
And once again Jack's behavior was
pushing Hope into Guy's arms.
Would this time be forever?

Watch for:
#1836 THE STRENGTH OF DESIRE
by Alison Fraser

Available in September wherever
Harlequin books are sold.

Look us up on-line at: http://www.romance.net